LONG GONE DADDIES

LONG GONE DADDIES

a novel

by David Wesley Williams

JOHN F. BLAIR, PUBLISHER
Winston-Salem, North Carolina

Published by
JOHN F. BLAIR,
P U B L I S H E R
1406 Plaza Drive
Winston-Salem, North Carolina 27103
www.blairpub.com

The first chapter appeared in a different form in *The Common* (2011, Issue No. 2).
www.davidwilliamsauthor.com
http://davidwwilliams.blogspot.com (The Soundcheck & the Fury)
http://twitter.com/damnshortstory

Jacket image ©Tatiana Popova/Used under license from Shutterstock.com
Jacket design by Brooke Csuka

Library of Congress Cataloging-in-Publication Data

Williams, David Wesley.
  Long Gone Daddies : a novel / by David Wesley Williams.
      p.   cm.
  ISBN 978-0-89587-593-8 (alk. paper) — ISBN 978-0-89587-594-5 (ebook) 1.
Rock groups—Fiction. 2. Musical fiction. I. Title.
  PS3623.I5564955L66 2013
  813'.6—dc23
                                    2012029225

10 9 8 7 6 5 4 3 2 1

To my wife, Barbara, our son, Adam,
and my parents, Joseph and the late Joyce Williams.

Thanks to my compatriots in the Moss Workshop in Fiction
at the University of Memphis.

Thanks to John F. Blair, Publisher, and particularly to my editor,
Steve Kirk.

Table of Contents

Author's Note

This is a work of fiction, set in some very real places, namely Memphis and the Mississippi Delta. Likewise, the characters are fictional, except when they're not—Elvis Presley appears as a busboy, and the bluesman Furry Lewis as a ghost. The first may have happened in real life; the second is a regular occurrence, Memphis being a city of many ghosts.

As for time, there are two main storylines. One runs mostly in 1953, between the death of Hank Williams and the rise of Elvis, when the music of the American South was catching its breath; the other is set forty-some years later, when Memphis was in a funk from which it has since awakened. The hallowed site of Stax Records, for example, is no longer the empty lot that it is in these pages, and was in those times, but is rather home to the Soulsville Charter School, the Stax Music Academy, and the Stax Museum of American Soul Music.

Memphis reborn? Nah, Memphis never dies. Sometimes, you just have to listen harder to hear it.

Soundcheck

Elvis Presley was a mama's boy grown up strange, a public-housing scourge in pink with an oil drip. But he had those hips and he had that voice. Carl Perkins heard it from over in Jackson and he made fast for Memphis.

They all did. Memphis called out and they came. Memphis was a song on the radio and they wanted some. They came to Sun Records to see Mr. Sam Phillips, and their wide eyes met his wild ones, their pleas fell on his cocked ear. They were young and dirt-poor and not averse to a better life through song. It beat chopping cotton or driving a truck or whatever else they'd done to turn dimes to dollars.

So out of Arkansas came Johnny Cash, sounding like doom looked. He had a voice of deep, swaggering sadness and wanted to sing gospel, but it was train tracks and prison bars instead. Jerry Lee Lewis, all piss and high-test, strode up from Louisiana with a piano on his back, keys aflame, just to show all those guitar players it didn't have to be wood to burn. There were others from elsewhere. There was Charlie Feathers, like Elvis a

Mississippi boy. Charlie Feathers—where'd he pick up that name, the pawnshop? But he may have whipped them all with "Defrost Your Heart," a spooky-sad country croon like something out of the Hank canon.

Memphis called out and they came. Memphis was a song on the radio and they wanted some. They came to Sun Records to see Mr. Sam Phillips. He took them in and together they cut records of uncommon scruff and joy.

That's their story. This is ours—my family's. We went to church on those songs, three generations living and dying by the music of Memphis, the Mississippi Delta, and all of the South. They were gifts from the gods, those songs. They were sacred things to us.

And this is the story of another. She went to the bank on those songs, to plunder the music for what gold it might give her.

But the songs know. The songs decide.

Here's one for you. It goes something like this . . .

PART I

Special Riders

1

Some nights, we have the road to ourselves and the radio sings only for us. We play our shows and tear-ass out. Tonight, it was this little dive bar in a town we took to calling East Motherless—nobody there but two old boys shooting pool for beers and a long-haul trucker we all swore was dead. One night, we played to an empty room, couldn't even scare up a ghost. But we play, no matter. We rock and then we roll. The soundcheck and the fury, the power chord and the glory. Then we load our gear into a muddy-brown Merc with a little trailer behind, and we're off. Slinging gravel, filling sky with road.

Buck Walker drives and plays drums. He's got a heavy foot and club hands, but he keeps the beat. Jimmy Lee Vine's on electric guitar. That's him in the backseat, wrapped like cable around a woman he met in a phone booth outside of another Texas town. We give names to all of the little towns and that was Eden. It was ramshackle buildings on hardscrabble streets, but then you should have seen Beulah Land.

The woman's name is Delia. I've yet to catch her last name or she's yet to say it. She says she can sing and she wants to see the world. She scares me something crucial. My name is Luther Gaunt. It's me riding shotgun and playing the old family guitar—Cassandra is her name—and thinking way too much. I write the songs and sing them. I was singing one tonight when I sensed something behind. If I looked, I'd have seen that our new bass player decided all on her own, in mid-song, to join the band. But I kept singing, lost to the song, eyes open just enough to make me wonder what took those two old boys from their game of stick and made that trucker rise from the dead.

The songs are in the guitar, a 1930s Cassandra Special Rider the color of whiskey and water. It was my daddy's, and before that it was his daddy's, and before that it was a birch tree. There's a scroll of gold flowers around the sound hole—an offering, my daddy said, to the dark hollow within.

My daddy told me a good many things, for never being around much. He told me stories of the road and the songs he found there. Songs of sweet evil and blue ruckus. Murder ballads, odes to ghosts. Drinking hymns.

I didn't believe everything he said—I've got a mother, too—but some of those things were true and some were even wise. Some were both, like how the songs come through the sound hole at the strum of chords, the slide of fingers across strings.

The songs flow like river and drink. They pour forth like smoke signals, factory steam.

My daddy and his would follow that Cassandra guitar anywhere. They were dust upon the land, singers in search of song. Always, there was a song whispering to them.

"Sweet talk and come-ons, Luther," my daddy, John Gaunt,

said. "Secret chords, mystery tunings. You understand what I'm saying, boy?"

I was *boy* and *son* and sometimes *Luther* to him. I was his best audience, a packed house, ever rapt. I hung on every word and bought the tour T-shirt. I said I thought so, maybe, and my daddy said, "Well, you will."

I think about that as I pick the strings of the old Cassandra guitar. I pluck and strum. My thumb drums soft on her body. I'm not so much at playing the thing. I'm no god. I'm not my daddy, the sly wonder. He could make that guitar sound like a train, a chicken, or any damn thing—bedsprings at midnight or a battle-field at dawn.

"Make it sound like a train, Daddy," I'd say.

"The Cotton Blossom or the Sunnyland?"

He knew all the rail lines, every one sounding like some made-up name. I'd pick one.

"The Twin-Star Rocket," I'd say.

"Oh, damn, boy. That's a fine one."

He'd play some song and then say to me, always, "My daddy was better. My daddy was the best—and the world would have known it, too. But things happened, Luther. He was supposed to go and record for Mr. Sam Phillips at Sun Records in Memphis. This was 1953, before Elvis and 'That's All Right.' You see what I'm getting at, son?"

I nodded like I knew, and my daddy said, "He had a song worked up with a couple of boys he played with. Mr. Sam, see, he was looking for a white man could sing black. He said he could make a billion dollars with that man. This is history, Luther. It happened. Mr. Sam, he thought your granddaddy Malcolm Gaunt might have been the one."

I was just a boy, but I knew these stories were more than

mere truth. I knew myths and legends when I heard them. They were songs to me, all of them, and I hung from every hook.

"A man working for Mr. Sam, he heard my daddy play in this Memphis club called the Eagle's Nest. Came up to him after and said something like, '*Damn*, man.' Then he told Malcolm to come see Mr. Sam. He said what day to be there. So my daddy, your granddaddy, he didn't come begging like Johnny Cash did later, like Carl Perkins and Jerry Lee Lewis. I'm not saying there's a thing wrong with begging for what you want. Some men, though, history taps on their shoulder and asks please. But like I said, Luther boy, things happened." It was like one of those moments of silence in church or before a ball game after somebody big has died, the way he paused. "Well, they sure as hell did that day."

"What happened, Daddy?"

"It was the morning of the day," he'd say, and then say no more. He'd take up the guitar instead. He'd play a little of nothing in particular, just something to fill the air and the moment with a sound other than words. Because words failed, just then. Because how do you tell a boy that his granddaddy—the family ideal, the best of them all, maybe better even than Elvis and the rest—never played a note for Mr. Sam Phillips at Sun Records because he was shot and killed for taking up with some other man's wife?

There's a picture of him standing out front of the train station in Memphis. It was 1953. He had made many trips down south from his home up north, but this was his last. He stood outside of Central Station, guitar case at his feet, cigarette on his lips. He looked weary from the haul, but he was working on a smile as the picture was snapped. Could be he liked what he could see of the woman behind the camera.

There's a second picture from just moments later. Malcolm had loosened his bones, become his old self again. He'd let his arms drop to his sides, let his fingers dangle. Malcolm's fingers were long and thin like the fringe on some old cowboy singer's stage shirt. Malcolm's fingers were endless, my daddy said, like the road and some women's legs. My daddy's fingers weren't nearly so long, and mine are even less so. Sometimes, I can't help but feel like the last of a diminishing line.

What to do, I wonder, but play it out?

So Malcolm left home that last time. He left the gray, be-smoked North for the bright, sunny South, first by foot and then by hitching and finally by train. I wonder was it the Pan American, the one Hank Williams sang about. I wonder was it the Mystery Train.

Some things I know for sure: Malcolm left a wife back home in Pennsylvania, in the coal-dusted city of Scranton. Sara was her name. I spent many an hour with her. I was the only one who would. Everybody said Sara was bone-mean and the reason Malcolm wandered, but I knew better, even as a boy who knew practically nothing else. I knew because by then I'd heard the songs. I was starting to understand already, like my daddy said I would.

I'd found the old records. I had to root in closets and cellars, but they called to me. I heard them through floorboards, in dreams. I followed the sound and found them, records black as country midnight. And me, scared of the dark—and drawn to it.

My daddy said it was always this way. Back to the bogs of Ireland, he said, the men of the Gaunt line followed the songs. They followed them onto ships bound for America. In the New World, the songs settled in the mountains and later set out on foot for the cities. They met and mingled with the blues. They woke in strange beds and stirred to strange sounds. There were songs about every moving thing. Songs about fast trains and big rivers. Songs about songs. Sad songs, too, about love and last call. He played them all for me. Bad things happened in those songs. Love went south and turned dark: Knives were unsheathed and shown to fair maiden skin; the skin did not flinch, but it bled when cut. Shootings and drownings. Rain by the torrent, high water everywhere. The world would come just shy of ending, and most always there was a woman, a wife, back home. Sometimes, there would even be a song about her, but only sometimes.

My daddy told me all this, and me just a boy. My grandmother Sara told me the same stories, but set to different music.

"The family name was Gaughan," she said. "But then America got a good look and called them Gaunt. It happened like that sometimes, Luther. Those Irish didn't care. You could call them anything. They were just glad to be in some new place. My people were Irish, too. But different stock. I was a Power. My people got to keep that name in America. I guess it was one America could spell."

The Powers were a stout line, the way Sara told it. I made them even more so in my mind—shoulders wide as church doorways and chests broad as whiskey barrels. I loved the tales of the scoundrel Gaunts with their guitars and songs, but I needed to know about the Powers, too. I needed to know that such people existed. So I begged her for stories and she told me a few. These were not myths and legends, but dispatches from a time and a place and what happened there. They had the heft of truth, the stench of sweat.

"The thing of it is, Luther," my grandmother Sara said, "the name Power means 'the poor man.' Lord knows, my people were poor. They were poor as those Gaunts were gaunt. But the Powers, they worked. Lord, boy, they did."

The Powers were given broad shoulders as their stake in the world, but the barrel chests they came by honestly. They earned every pence and shilling they were given and every pound they were denied. Then it was pennies and nickels and the odd dollar.

"The New World didn't change them one," she said.

"One what, Grandmother?"

"Iota. You know what that is, Luther?"

I just listened for what she'd say.

"It's even less than a little bit." The old woman sighed and looked off into the distance, as if the past might come cresting now over Grove Street hill, a lunchpail in one hand and a miner's helmet in the other. "It's hardly more than none at all."

"Iota," I said.

"It's how they measure truth and love and money, and a few other things, probably, that just never seem to add up to enough," she said. "They don't teach you that in school, but I'm telling you now."

My grandma Sara Gaunt could be mean, it's true. My daddy said it and she did, too, in her way. She rode her boy hard. He said it was like he'd been born with the Gaunt version of original sin—Malcolm's trespasses heaped upon him. She all but pushed him out the door, he said, with that guitar in his hands.

But the old woman liked me. I listened to her. I wanted to hear her version of the truth, the ring and toll of it. I collected versions of the truth the way other boys did baseball cards.

"Grandmother, what became of my granddaddy?"

We'd sit in the front room of her little house near the foot of Grove Street hill, an alley-shot from where I lived with my mother. She sat in an old straight-back wooden chair with a Bible on the table beside her. She'd pick it up from time to time. She never opened it, that I saw. It might as well have been a wooden carving of a Bible. She'd just shake it at me. She'd say, "Are you a God-fearing boy?"

Sara Gaunt was a substantial woman, tall enough to look any Gaunt man in his wandering eyes. Her own eyes seemed closer to gray than any other color and her body was a rigid thing of the ironworks. People wondered what must have possessed that handsome guitar slinger Malcolm Gaunt to marry such a cold, mean, straight-up-and-down woman. But I knew because I'd seen the pictures. They were in the sleeves of the records I found. They were young then, Malcolm and Sara, slow-dancing in a barroom, him in a suit and her in a dress, his arm slung low across her backside, like a swipe that lingered. You didn't have to play those records to hear the music they danced to, but I did. I played those records every chance.

There was another picture. They were around a table with friends, glasses raised and faces grinning. Sara's face was half-hidden by her long curls of hair. And another picture, taken by a lake. It was summer and Sara had been swimming. She was posing for the camera, summer-vamping, hands through those sopping curls and hip jutting.

The young Mrs. Malcolm Gaunt had curves like that Cassandra Special Rider guitar.

I take a drink and pass the bottle to the backseat, to Delia there. She takes a sip and chases it with a swig.

"Cheap stuff," she says.

"House brand of the night, my daddy used to say."

"Your daddy said a great many things, sounds like. He liked to talk."

"He did more. He wrote songs and sang them. He went out into the world."

"Well, I don't remember the name. I don't guess he made it big."

"No, Delia. I don't guess he did."

I turn in the seat to watch her drink. She takes another sip, another swig. She lowers the bottle. Her lips glisten, wet with nectar and that hooch. She hands back the bottle.

"You think making it big is the measure of a man, Delia? You think the point of writing a song is for the world to hear it and turn it into some big smash? You think fame's the only thing, the whole point of it all?"

"Yeah to all that," she says.

I take a drink and hand her the bottle again. She raises it as if to toast me, but she says, "I scare the hell out of you, don't I, Luther Gaunt?"

I'm honest, on top of thinking way too much.

"Oh, hell yeah, Delia."

When the weather was good, we'd sit out on the porch. My grandmother Sara would trade her straight-back chair and shaken Bible for a rocker and fly swatter. But her stories—of the families, the Powers and the Gaunts—were much the same. They were parables, I guess you'd say. I was to learn from them. They were to scare me.

She told me of the Gaunts, with those songs in their heads, and of the Powers, with miners' helmets on theirs. She said the families had a habit of marrying, said it was the way of the fates. She said the Gaunts were good looking even in their gauntness, with thick heads of black hair and eyes dark as notes on sheet music. She said they dressed as slick as they could afford, and then some, and that they had a way that worked like potion on those female Powers.

"Most men those Power girls knew, they looked like they'd been coughed up out of the ground," she said. "But you couldn't get a Gaunt to go down so much as the basement's steps. They wouldn't have gone into a mine if you told them it was songs they'd be mining." Something almost like a smile caught her unaware. She didn't fight it too awfully hard. "But they had a way about them," she said. "And you know"—wistfully, she said it; she looked away so I couldn't see her face—"they had such . . . Well, it was nice, how they sang."

"Is that how it was with you and my granddaddy?" I said.

She sat rocking just slightly on the front porch. She sat watching the day and did not say anything for the longest time. Then she said, "Your mother will be starting dinner, Luther. You best go and help her."

"So did my granddaddy have that thick head of hair and those dark eyes"—I must have sounded wistful then, but at boy speed, hopped up on knowing that all my memories were ahead of me—"and did he play that guitar and sing you songs?"

"I hear your mother calling."

I dropped my head. I made a move to stand. I said, "Grandmother?"

"You best go and help her. I don't intend to tell you again."

"What happened to keep Granddaddy Malcolm from going to see Mr. Sam Phillips at Sun Records?"

"You want to get whipped by me and your ma both, Luther?"

But I heard something in her voice, or something missing. I said, "What happened on the morning of the day, Grandmother?"

She waved the fly swatter. She shook her head. "Most boys your age, they just want to know what's going to happen next. Get your head out of the cobwebs, Luther Gaunt."

But I knew she wasn't about to banish me. I knew because

I'd seen those old pictures and I'd heard those old songs. She knew it, too. She could see it on my face, reflected. That's how it seemed to me, and me just a boy then. She was that young, curvy thing again. She had those wild curls of hair and Malcolm was there, arm slung low across her backside. A song played. They danced.

"What happened on the morning of the day, Grandmother?" I said, trying to bring her back.

She just looked at me, said nothing. Because how do you tell a boy that his granddaddy had been in that woman's bed when her husband arrived with his gun to shoot them both?

Back in Arkansas, a muddy-brown Mercury with Pennsylvania plates and a little trailer behind drifts off the shoulder of a two-lane back road. If this place had a name, it might be Indifference. If the shoulder could, it would shrug.

"Buck! Hey, goddamn, Buck!"

This is me, shouting to no avail. Buck is driving, but Buck is sleeping, and so the car bounds into the ditch and out again. The Merc is airborne now, that most primitive of rocket ships in the Arkansas night sky. But as the ditch belched it out, gravity snatches it back.

A thudding crash, a chorus of curses, and still Buck sleeps.

The car hurtles across an abandoned rice field, over rut and furrow and—

"Fuuuuuck!"

The woods are just ahead, the Merc about to crash. I think to pray, but what prayer begins with *Fuuuuuck*?

But something happens—or rather, nothing does. Seems we're not about to die after all. That just won't do, before we've even cut a record, or Delia has seen the world east of the Mississippi. We must suffer more—so many small deaths and indignities, the back of fate's hand, luck's boot, maybe even some comeuppance. Then, maybe, posterity will come around for a sniff at the likes of us, the Long Gone Daddies.

And so, good people:

The car gives out, choking on its fumes. The engine dies with a shudder and a wheeze in the moon shadows of the woods.

2

Malcolm Gaunt walked into a Scranton bar early one summer day in 1953. It was Souse Milton's, a long, narrow drinking hall, dark as a confessional even on this bright morning. It had a plank-wood floor and a pressed-tin ceiling and a tin-topped counter that ran nearly the length of the place. At the far end, a newspaperman sat talking to an off-duty cop. A couple was at a table in front; the man was shrugging and the woman's eyes were rolling. They seemed to have been out all night and over its course had developed the ability to argue without talking.

Souse Milton was at the tap. He looked up when the door opened. He said nothing, just looked for some nothing to do, a glass to wash.

"Souse," Malcolm said in his best hail-fellow tone.

Souse just nodded.

"So it's like that," Malcolm said, and then, "Short glass of beer for your best enemy, then. And what the hell, a round for the house."

I would make stories of Malcolm—not make up, as in fiction, but piece together, as if in fact. I wanted to know who my granddaddy was and where he went and what he did there. I wanted to know why. I took what little my grandmother Sara would tell me, and my daddy's secondhand version, too. I talked to anybody who knew him. I listened to those old records and looked at the old pictures. Read some letters. Newspaper clippings, too.

I was putting together a puzzle—a map of the world, a portrait of the artist as a lousy spouse and long gone daddy—from a thousand little bits of broken whiskey-bottle glass.

Malcolm settled himself at the bar, his guitar case stretched across two stools to his right. He said to the off-duty cop with a nod, "I didn't do it, copper," and to the newspaperman with a wink, "It's like I told Scranton's finest, there. But you're free to print whatever will sell a rag or two. Frankly, I could use the press."

"Ha," said the cop, tall and thin, like he'd become his own night stick. "Crime's too much like work for you, Malcolm Gaunt."

The scribe was a squat man with an oversized head who had worked for the local rag so long he spoke in headlines: "Singer slays crowd; five dead."

Malcolm smiled and turned toward the couple at the table up front. He wanted to see what would come of their silent dispute. He wanted to see if there might be a song in it.

The woman was standing now, hands on hips. She wore a shabby dress of faded red. Malcolm said, "Garnet? Burgundy?"

He was trying to make the shade of the dress. He was hoping for something that would rhyme with something else. He said, "Well, it ain't fire-engine red."

"I'd say more the fire than the engine," the cop said.

"Three-alarm dress," the newspaperman said. "All perish."

"Damn, boys, those are lines to a song. Mind if I cop 'em?"

Souse Milton washed a highball glass and said without looking up, "You always did just take what you wanted, Malcolm Gaunt."

"Damn, Souse. Give a man a break."

Souse thought maybe an arm, the right, the one the son of a bitch used to strum and pick that old guitar—it was already an old guitar in '53. Souse smiled at the thought, and then just smiled. He was no better at holding a grudge than at fighting the cause of it.

"Well," he said, and leaned on the bar as they all watched the table up front. Something seemed about to happen. The beset man was slightly built and had something of a pompadour. He wore black trousers and a white shirt about half-tucked. He waved the woman away. She sat, arms crossed.

Souse said, "I'll take them those beers you bought and see about that shade of red. Maybe it'll be something you can rhyme up and set to music and make a thousand bucks on. You could pay your old tab, far as it would go."

Souse pulled the tap and filled two short glasses. He delivered them to the table. He said they were courtesy of the no-good musician at the bar.

The man took one of the glasses and raised it to Malcolm. He took a drink and set it down, tried for a satisfied smile. The woman took her beer and doused the man with it. She stood again. Her hands were raised to her hips. The man sputtered, trying to speak.

Souse Milton stood by watching and then went for a bar rag.

"Damn it to hell, woman," the man managed to say.

Now she took the other beer. They all watched as she raised the glass. The newspaperman reached, from habit, for his notebook, and the off-duty cop for his absent night stick. Rhymes ran through Malcolm's head and Souse breathed the sigh of a man who had seen too much drama for one day, and it barely ten o'clock in the morning.

"Woman douses man a second time," the scribe said. "Twenty dollars says so."

"Nah, don't think so. Man can't drown but once," the cop said. "But I'll gladly take your ink-stained money, wretch."

Malcolm smiled. He knew. He could about set it to taps on the tin-topped bar. He watched as the woman raised that beer to her lips, and he said, gazing at her thrown-back head and a neck so bare it seemed an indecency even for a dark Scranton bar, "God, but I love to watch a woman drink."

The woman drained the beer and then slammed the glass on the table and made to leave. The man was on her heels; they were red to match her dress, her lips, her nature. The man made to stop her.

The scribe handed the cop a ten and said, "I'll have to owe you the rest."

The cop said, "Yepper, you will."

The man was a step slow and so got a mouthful of door when she slammed it. He stood there for the longest time holding his jaw, as if otherwise it would fall in forty-some-odd pieces to the plank-wood floor.

He turned to the men and said, "Did you ever see the like?"

The men all said they had.

"Hey, Luther, man?"

"Yeah, Jimmy Lee?"

"Care to make yourself scarce, brother? Give me and my girl Delia here some privacy?"

"Sure, Jimmy Lee."

I make myself scarce. I step outside the car. I lie across the hood with the old guitar on top—Cassie's like Delia, she likes to be on top—and my beer within reach. I pick, I strum, I drum that thumb. But I can't conjure a song, mine or anybody else's, and so I sit in darkest Arkansas and drink from the snub-nosed brown bottle.

I close my eyes and try for some old radio song. It's Johnny Cash, his voice a low rumble like God with a chest cold, singing about a woman named Delia. There are hundreds of songs about women named Delia—or maybe just the one song about a single woman, sung hundreds of ways. There was Blind Willie McTell's Delia; she got herself shot, too, just like Johnny's. I wonder if our Delia might be the one to write a new ending to the old song.

Delia, Delia, Delia.

I say her name, half-sing it. I drift to silence. I watch the sky, black and empty, an unsung song about a woman named—

Then, out of nowhere, or east of there, come fireworks, all thump and glow. Lines of light collide and splinter, sparks trail. The sky is a-bloom, the sky is a-sputter, and I trace the designs left by the fading lines—that's my favorite part, the fading away. I close my eyes, open them—close and open, close and open, and every time a new sky, neon-dusted.

Damn, I'd forgotten. It's the Fourth of July.

I watch in wonder. I think of home, rare moments there. When my rambling daddy was off the road, he'd put his cigarette lighter to a Roman candle and say he was giving God a hotfoot.

My mother would stand in the doorway and watch. I'd smile up at her.

Close and open, close and open. Now the sky is filled with some new language, a message. An old story or my fate foretold, I couldn't begin to say.

We're going to Memphis, the sacred muck, the shining jewel of all sad backwaters. We're going to Memphis, great lost city of sound. You can walk on whiskey in Memphis. You can bang your blue guitar.

"Your guitar," says the city on the bluff to the pilgrim at the banks of the big river, "is it blue?"

Pilgrim says, "Oh, it's sad as can be."

We're going to Memphis to become famous or something like it, to be discovered and cut a record, to do as Elvis did, and B. B. King and the Howlin' Wolf, Johnny Cash and my daddy's favorite, Carl Perkins, and a million blue others.

We're broken down in an abandoned Arkansas rice field just now, with no apparent way to get back on the road, much less down it.

But what the hell? We're forty-odd years late already.

3

When I came of age, I would sit in Souse Milton's, talking to the old bartender. He would pour short glasses of beer and tell stories. Most days, he couldn't stop talking, and then something—a memory, maybe—would catch him funny, the way that smile did my grandmother that day. Then he wouldn't say anything but, "Well." We'd just sit in silence or I'd play the jukebox.

Souse told all about the human drama he'd seen and sopped up in bar rags and wrung out. He told of women in shabby red dresses and disheveled men with pompadours. He told of coal miners, too, and how hard they drank. They'd break into song late at night. There was a group of them, he said, called themselves the Black Lung Boys. He said they sang old miners' songs and I thought of my grandmother Sara's people and their like, coughed up out of the ground.

Souse would pour himself a glass and come around to the drinking side of the tin-topped counter. We were a pair. I was freshly legal in a backward ball cap, and Souse an old man with a thick head of white hair. I was a Gaunt to my restless bones, but I think he saw some hope for me yet. Hell, though: Old Souse Milton was a bartender who'd outlived all his regulars. He wanted to talk, needed to talk; he'd have told those tales to the walls, though they knew them, every one.

"Play the jukebox, Luther boy," he said one day, "and I'll tell you about the woman."

He said it like she was the only one God made.

I lie on the hood of the Merc. I sleep and dream. It's the usual one, my worst fears done up newsreel style: Patsy Cline's splintered cheekbones and Otis Redding's charred flesh, Buddy Holly's smashed glasses. Planes crashing and singers dying, everything blood-red that's not smoke-gray. But it's the silence afterward that gets me.

I wake up to Delia standing there.

"Dreaming about me?"

I don't say anything, and then I say, "Patsy Cline."

"Hmm." She says it as if Patsy were that rarest sort of rival to her—worthy.

"I was thinking about the day she died. Patsy. Otis and Buddy Holly, too. It's like God's got this thing against singers getting too high and mighty."

"God," Delia says, as if she's heard the name but can't place it.

"I'm thinking cars are the way to go."

I slide off the hood and she kicks the bumper pretty near to where I stand. "Well, it's true we're safe in this heap." She looks up, scans the sky, shrugs. "Unless, of course, some plane load of rock stars falls from the sky and crashes on us. Wouldn't that just be the damn way?"

She lifts the hood and looks at me, as if to say, *You're a man, right? Fix it.*

I look at the belts and valves and hoses, something that might be a pump. *I'm a musician*, I want to say. *I can write you a song about a car, but you're strictly on your own making the thing go.*

"Maybe that gasket's bad," I say, pointing with my bottle.

"Yeah," Delia says, laughing. "It thinks it's the oil filter."

"What do you know about cars?"

"I had a boyfriend," she says. "Real gear head. Thought all the action was under the hood. And there I was in the backseat, not a stitch on."

"You say shit just to get to me, don't you, Delia?"

"I get to you just standing here, Luther. I don't have to say a word."

What do I even say? My car's dead, my band's stranded, and a woman in full torment mode is standing beside me in cutoff jeans, a T-shirt that tells me to go to hell because I'm not from Texas, and black engineer boots she might have pulled off Casey Jones's corpse when it was still smoking. I shrug in lieu of shouting for help. Poor man's semaphore, I guess.

Patsy Cline, my one true carnal desire, was on her way back to Nashville from a show. That's when she crashed and died. They're always on their way home from a show, or on to the next one. The show was in Kansas City and the plane stopped for fuel in the little Tennessee town of Dyersburg, north of Memphis.

Patsy's plane crashed outside another little Tennessee town, Camden. It wasn't far from one to the other, but like my daddy told me one time, "Everywhere's a quick trip, boy, when you're going straight down."

Patsy Cline, Patsy Cline
There's no more to this song
just the one line

Goddamn, Patsy's voice: the way it would climb way up high and then go clear down and growl for you. That sad, deep, and perfect ache. I like her early stuff best, when they were still letting her be a cowgirl. But I like it all. She was thirty when she died. It was 1963. Long before my time, like most of what moves me.

> *Patsy Cline, Patsy Cline*
> *Can we go walkin' after midnight?*
> *Can you give me a sign?*

It's a country shuffle, my song about Patsy. Jimmy Lee won't like it. Jimmy Lee wants to crank up the guitars and make noise. He has a bit of the punk in him, a bit of outrage. He wants to be heard in border countries, feared throughout the land. He mooned a state trooper outside Fort Worth, but the trooper didn't notice. Or maybe mooning is legal in Texas. It's a different world down there, another country. Maybe Buck's evasive driving saved us. Maybe there's an APB out on James Lee Vine's pale cheeks. I smile at the thought, imagining the wanted poster in the post office.

Jimmy Lee does everything literally. I tend toward the figurative; it's a way to show my ass and keep my pants on.

I think of Patsy singing "Turn the Cards Slowly." It's one of those old country numbers. It's one where she growls, and then does this quick little whoop of a thing with her voice, like she's swallowed a yodel. Jesus, but I do have it bad for Patsy. Maybe Delia has a voice just like her, and then Jimmy Lee will go along with this country shuffle I seem to be writing. Or maybe Delia has a soul shout. I'd like that, too. We could sing a duet. I'd be Otis the king and she'd be my queen Carla Thomas, like on those old Stax soul records out of Memphis. Our stage show could use some sass and royalty.

> *Patsy Cline, Patsy Cline*
> *Have you met Otis?*
> *Have you sung "These Arms of Mine"?*

Otis Redding. The sound of a heart dredged dry. To sound like Otis, to move like Otis as the horns played behind him, woozy from trying to keep up. Otis moved like a preacher in a knife fight. Nobody moved like that. Nobody sang like that. Otis could have played a strip joint and he would've had all eyes on him. Otis stripped himself another kind of bare.

I move like a spilled drink. I fling myself across the stage. Other times, I stand stone-still, one foot forward like a drunk testifying. My front foot goes tap and tamp.

Otis's plane went down in a Wisconsin lake, December 1967. For Buddy Holly, it was February, snow, Iowa cornfield, 1959.

I'm alive and well, unknown and safe. So are we all. The Long Gone Daddies go by muddy-brown Merc or we don't go at all— all lurch and hurdle, getting off the ground for only the briefest of moments, staying under the radar of the Texas Highway Patrol and God alike.

Mid-morning. I'm watching Delia poke at the engine with a stick. Well, I'm watching Delia just generally.

"My last name is Shook," she says. "But I'm thinking of changing it to Shake."

"Always live in the present, I say."

But just because I say it doesn't mean I believe it.

Late morning. I sit on the bumper and strum the guitar. Delia lies on the hood and sighs. I think she might take up my song. I think I might finally hear her sing. But the only other sound is the faint rumble of far-off thunder.

"How's that sky look, Delia?"

Delia doesn't say. But I well could guess. Overcast, with a chance of falling rock stars.

4

"We were a couple of outlaws, me and your grand-daddy," Souse Milton said. "We thought we were."

I was piecing together the story of Malcolm's last trip south, in 1953. But now Souse jumped time on me. He said I needed to hear about that first trip, some fifteen years before. He said I needed to hear about the guitar, and about the woman. Then he went silent and I played the jukebox and waited. It was two days, but the music was good and the beer was cold and I was young. I could wait.

The jukebox sang about a sweet old world and something in the night. The jukebox sang about lost highways and mansions on the hill. The jukebox was one of the new ones, but it had an old soul. I filled it with my collection. Nobody came to the bar anymore, not even the man whose job it was to stock the jukebox.

Late afternoon on the second day, I poured us fresh beers and said, "So this one's about the start of it all. This one's about the woman."

"It is, but in good time," he said. "Be patient, Luther Gaunt. You're young and can't wait. I'm old and can't hurry. And anyway, you ought to know, as the latest in a long line of guitar players: The star never opens the show."

"Okay. So it's you and my granddaddy Malcolm. Couple of outlaws, you say."

I grinned, felt like a boy again. Old Souse shrugged.

"We were like brothers back then," he said. "We were young and skinny and some wild. Well, Malcolm was wild and I had my moments. This was our home base, this bar. My daddy owned it. They called him Souse, too. He didn't drink much by Scranton standards, but that's what they called him. He was a sensible man, my father. This was his job, was all. This is what he did. He was a good man. He was gentle with us kids. He never struck my mother. He spent long days and even longer nights right here where I stand. My daddy and now me. Lord, Luther, the days and the nights. I don't care to know how many. I don't guess he kept count either. Or maybe they all just added up to one. And after a day like that, he'd need to sleep off all that standing, and so his time with us was scarce. But he gave us what he had to give. I'm not talking only about food on the table."

"Good man, your father."

"Yes, good man," Souse said. "But you know the thing about good. Other men don't trust it. They figure a good man's got to be up to something. They wonder what. So they called him Souse to bring him down to their level, make him one of them, no better. And women, you know they prefer the outlaw, real or not. Your granddaddy Malcolm and I saw that. We took right naturally to it, too. Well, Malcolm did, and I took to Malcolm.

"So this one night, sitting there where you're sitting, he decided it. Lord, I can see us now. Malcolm, see, he would make up songs. He didn't have a guitar, but he'd grab one the old coal miners, those Black Lung Boys, kept around. He seemed to know how to play it just naturally. Damnedest thing, it was. His fingers, they just fell right into playing. And he had a voice for singing and a way with words. The girls, well, they liked it."

Souse Milton poured two more and walked around to join me. He settled onto a barstool. He said, "So the girls gathered around Malcolm to the point where his best buddy, who couldn't carry a tune, could get what they call action. Do they still call it action?"

I said I'd heard secondhand talk of such things, and Souse said, "But there was a problem. Good thing, too, or else we wouldn't have a story, would we, Luther Gaunt?"

I smiled and the old man sighed and the jukebox sang. It sang about a misguided angel. It sang about stolen cars and thick smoke, hungry eyes, and big legs in tight skirts.

"So there was a problem," I said.

"Right, right. Malcolm didn't have a guitar or the money to buy one. He was working some odd jobs but not earning much more than beer money. There was some cash to be made by crawling into those holes in the ground. But Malcolm, hell, he wasn't about to take up with those Black Lung Boys."

The old bartender told of them. They'd be in the back of the bar, good and lit, singing their old miners' songs. I'd heard them, growing up. They were mighty anthems. They were brave and desperate and sometimes somber, those songs, sounded like the earth groaning.

"You couldn't hear those old miners' tunes and not be moved.

But not, you know, the way the girls wanted to be moved. Malcolm saw that." The old man smiled. Now he was grinning. He was young again.

I leaned over the counter to fill his glass. Souse went on with the story.

"Well, there were a few girls that 'The Miner's Doom' and 'The Avondale Mine Disaster' worked a spell on. But mostly, the girls were drawn to Malcolm. Because he sang about getting wild, going places. That was just what they wanted to hear. But there was that problem I told you about."

"The guitar."

"That's right. Malcolm said he needed a guitar to string those girls along proper. He was saying it one night when one of those girls said, 'Well, if you two are outlaws like you say, why don't you steal one?' Well, I laughed. I was the son of a sensible man, a good man. I was no thief. I didn't know what Malcolm might do to get what he wanted, how far he might go. So I laughed it off, thought they would, too. But Malcolm, well . . . Malcolm kissed that girl on her red lips. 'Marry me,' he said. 'Marry the hell out of me.' He liked to say things like that and the girls liked hearing it.

"Well, the next day, Malcolm stood outside a dry-goods store. I was there with him. A guitar was in the window. We went inside and Malcolm asked the man behind the counter if he carried any other guitars. He said the one in the window was fine, but he wanted something fancier. The man said no, the company that made that one made others, like one called the Cassandra Special Rider, but there wasn't much call locally for such a guitar. The man had a catalog with pictures.

"Malcolm said, 'Where's this company, the one makes the Cassandra Special Rider?' He was thinking maybe Italy or some other planet, probably. The man behind the counter said, 'Jersey City.' "

Souse Milton lifted his empty glass. I offered to refill it, but he waved me off. He sighed. "I'm tired from talking, Luther boy," he said. "Come back tomorrow. I'll tell you how we really were a couple of outlaws—for one night, at least. I'll tell you how we went to Jersey City to steal a guitar and more or less succeeded."

"And the woman," I said. "You'll tell me about her?"

"The woman, yes," he said. "Her."

5

Delia has this wild and endless dirty-blond hair in a style you might call, "Run Screaming for Your Lives, Boys." She has a long, full face with eyes like blue neon as seen through pouring rain; I wonder what besides pouring rain a boy might run through just to get to see them up close.

And Delia, she has ruby-red, painted-up lips, and those old engineer boots in black that clash right nicely, I guess you'd say, with the pink satin shirt she took off of Jimmy Lee. She stands near six feet, with those endless legs of hers.

I say all this not to romanticize the woman, or God forbid to objectify her. More in the way of an all-points bulletin.

Delia: "Are you scared of all women, Luther?"

Me: "No, just the scary ones."

We're sitting in the Merc, waiting out the rain. Jimmy Lee's sleeping and Buck's gone to find help, so it's just us, talking.

"So just what kind of band have I fallen in with?" she says in her breezy Texas twang.

"You might have asked that before you joined up," I say. "But like it says on the marquee, we're the Long Gone Daddies. We play rock 'n' roll. We're scavengers. That's why we came south, you know. This is where the songs are. They've always been here. Field chants and soul shouts, hillbilly croons and blue romps, those gospel moans. All that stuff Elvis took and made a beautiful mess of. All the . . ."

I turn in the seat in time to see the withering look Delia gives me. "The South," she says in her thickest Southernese. "Oh, good God. The almighty South. Just a-suffering through the days. Pining for old times best forgot. Nursing whiskey and a war grudge. That's what all y'all think."

I could get used to being interrupted by the sound of that voice. I wouldn't miss at all the missing *g* on the ends of certain words. I find myself wondering how it sounds all sleepy in the morning, how it sounds when she sings. But I stop all that wondering. She's with Jimmy Lee. That, and she scares me. More all the time, y'all. More all the time.

So I say, because I can change a subject with the best of men, "My daddy, you know, he wasn't so sweet on Elvis. Oh, he liked him and all. He knew down deep he was the best. My daddy said when Elvis sang 'That's All Right' back in '54 that God Himself had serious notions of abdication, and the devil, he went into advertising. But of all those old Sun Records rockabilly kings, my daddy's guy was Carl Perkins. He loved Carl doing those rave-up songs of his—songs he wrote and didn't have handed to him. Yeah, and the way he played guitar. Carl's guitar, it could power a train. Carl's guitar could bring the freight. My daddy said Carl could have been a Gaunt."

"Excuse me for saying, Luther," she says, "but wasn't Carl Perkins pretty near a one-hit wonder?"

I shrug and say, "Well, yeah. That's what cinched it for my

daddy, I guess. That's why Carl was his man. You might call it a character flaw, but my daddy didn't want to belong to the whole damn world. My daddy, after all, was the son of a man who might have been the biggest thing ever at Sun Records, except he never struck that first note in Mr. Phillips's studio."

"Yeah, yeah," Delia says. "You told me before. The morning of the day. Something happened, but you never did say what. But whatever it was—"

"Well, I was working up to that."

"—whatever it was, it wouldn't have stopped me."

"Well, you're of one stock and I'm of another, Delia. I'm not saying mine's better. I'm not saying yours wouldn't kick mine's ass in a fight. I don't know. It might have been Malcolm didn't have the gumption to make history. I can see how you value gumption, or whatever it is your stock calls it. Maybe Malcolm didn't have it, or have enough of it. I never knew the man. I just know him through the old stories, mostly. That's my knowledge of the family stock. You might call it lazy and say it lacks ambition. I won't disagree. But it's my stock, so I look for something good to take from it. Because I'm one of them. They're in me, parts of them, things that made them what they were. So I look for something to admire. And it's there. To me, it is. You've got to look hard, but there it is—integrity, of a sort. My daddy had it, all right."

"Integrity," Delia says, "of a sort."

"You couldn't orchestrate my daddy," I say. "He'd play his songs where he stood and sleep where he fell. Then he'd move on. You'd see him and then you wouldn't. He'd fall asleep in Jackson and wake up in Memphis. He wore the cover of darkness like Elvis wore those fancy, spangled capes of his." This is my version of my daddy, my vision of the man. It's mostly presumed and pieced together and wild-guessed, but I believe it's true. It is to me. "He didn't want riches and acclaim, the trappings of fame. He said to me, 'Luther, they're called *trappings* for a reason.'"

Delia shakes her head. "Or maybe he didn't . . . Oh, I don't know," she says. "Never mind. He's your daddy. Not like mine was any better."

"Or maybe my daddy didn't have what it took to make it big, you mean? Maybe he was the second coming of Carl Perkins, without a 'Blue Suede Shoes' to sing? Maybe he swore off what he couldn't have anyway?"

"Well?"

"That's occurred to me, yeah."

"You're just all the way a Gaunt, aren't you, Luther?" Delia says, as much to mock as to pity.

And so Souse Milton, a sensible man's son, a sensible man himself, told the story of the night he and my granddaddy Malcolm Gaunt drove to a guitar factory in Jersey City to steal a Cassandra Special Rider guitar.

"I was the brains. He was the light fingers. That's what Malcolm said, how he said it. I said, 'Well, that ought to have it covered.' But he said no. He said we'd have a third."

"Sara Power," I said.

"Yepper. She put us up to it. She was the one. I don't think she thought anybody was going to steal anything, but she wanted to go somewhere. She'd been out of Scranton only to go to the Jersey Shore. She wanted to see the world. She came from mining folk, you know. They were glad just to be on the upside of the earth's crust sometimes. Hell, they thought Scranton looked good. Didn't have much call to wander off to New York City and see if those buildings really did scrape the sky. So this would get her a couple of hundred miles down that road and into some danger, sidled up with a couple of so-called outlaws."

"You liked her."

"Hell," Souse Milton said, and then said no more for the rest of the morning.

The next day, Souse drew a beer for me, made a highball for himself. He said, "Let me tell you, Luther. I liked the fights. Boxing, you know. Joe Louis was my guy—right up until he became the champ. Then I had to throw him over for the challenger. Most of the time, anyway. I was a sucker for the underdog, see. I liked to bet, but I didn't squander much. I come from sensible stock, remember. And I liked that I would follow my father at the bar. I liked what he did for a living. I liked that he came to a place every morning and worked that place, served a purpose. He didn't care that his name was on the place. He didn't care for that name, particularly. But he liked that there was such a place and it was his. I liked that it would be mine. I liked my life, all right. And I liked my best buddy, Malcolm Gaunt, too, and his way with a song. There were some other things I guess I liked, too. But your grandma Sara Power? Nah."

"You loved her."

Souse Milton smiled. He was working on his second highball. He said, "So we were to set out from Scranton for Jersey City. I thought the first thing we'd have to do before we stole that Cassandra Special Rider was to steal a car, because I didn't have one and neither did Malcolm. But he came driving up to the bar that night—it was a Saturday, I'll never forget it—in an old Pontiac. I didn't know what damn fool he borrowed it from. I didn't know if the damn fool even knew he'd lent it.

"So we set out at midnight. Malcolm had this old empty guitar case in the backseat and he put it in the boot, so Sara could stretch out. She said she wanted to sleep and dream and wake up in a new place. She said we were to wake her when the bright lights of the big city came into view. Malcolm took to calling her 'honey babe.' He said, 'Honey babe, I'll show you the world. That guitar we're stealing will take us there.' She rolled her eyes at that, but she liked hearing it. I could tell because I watched her. I couldn't take my eyes off her. She was . . ."

The old man sighed. He seemed to look about for a word he could lift without too much strain. He finally just said, "She was the damnedest thing ever was."

"What was it about her?"

"You said you've seen old pictures of her, right? So you know the bombshell part. But it was more than that. She was brave and smart and wise and wild. I hadn't known all those things to come in a single person. But there she was: Sara. I knew she was too much woman for me. I thought she might be too much woman for Malcolm, even. I suppose by the end of this story you might wonder if she wasn't too much woman for herself, too."

"Malcolm liked her."

"He liked her, yeah. Loved her, even. But Malcolm was always falling in love. Hell, he'd dive right in. It was different with him. I swear, that man. Just by the force of his personality, that man attracted females by the flock. That will blind a person. I figure it would have blinded me. I wonder what good sense would do in the face of a whole flock of females. I'd maybe put my money on good sense, but only because I'm a sucker for the underdog, you know."

Souse Milton fought a smile to a draw. He said, "But I'm getting off track. Old men do that. Tomorrow, then, young Luther Gaunt, grandson of Malcolm?"

"Tomorrow, good man."

Half past four and Buck returns. He has a fifth of tequila and a rack of steer horns he's attaching to the hood with an ice pick and some speaker wire he found in the trunk. He's jabbing holes in the hood with the ice pick and stringing them through with the wire, as if the car died from the lack of horns.

Turns out there's gas in the tequila bottle and gas is what we need. Gas and steer horns. Buck cranks the car without saying a word, and after a series of hacking coughs it starts.

6

"So what became of your daddy?" Delia says. "And tell about your mama."

We've crept onto the highway, eastbound. Delia sounds like she's stuck watching a TV with just one channel, and that one channel doesn't beat much, but it beats the hell out of staring at Arkansas.

"Well, my mother is fine," I say. "I call her Ma. She's a good woman. She works in a bookstore. She lives up north, still. Scranton, you know. She stacks books on shelves and recommends books to people and mostly she reads. She likes adventure tales. I guess being married to one didn't turn her off them. Or maybe it's the other way around. She missed all the adventure, being married to the adventurer."

"I'd have left him cold," Delia says.

"I used to wonder about that. I wondered if she thought she could change him, or did she just love him no matter and so was willing to wait out his rambling? Their whole marriage some-times seemed to me a contest to see if she had more loving pa-tience than he had rambling fuel. They both ran on fumes a lot of the time, I think."

"I'd have left him cold."

"You mentioned that," I say. "I asked her one time if she ever thought of it. She said after a few years she did, then after a few more she decided there wasn't much of a point—she'd have to find the son of a bitch to leave him."

"So he beat her to that, too."

"Yeah, he did, Delia."

"So what became of him?"

"Well, that's the thing. I don't know. Ma doesn't."

My daddy would take off rambling, chasing skirt and song, drinking whatever. Whiskey was his choice, but he'd drink trans-mission fluid and run on that awhile. He'd find some new place all lush with song and then, just like that, he'd make like smoke. But he'd always come home, with Cass and the clothes on his back and next to nothing in his pockets, singing some sad tune. Ma would take him back. He was winning, in his way. So there'd be domestic bliss and a shut bedroom door for a few days, and late at night he'd sit out on the front stoop with me and tell sto-ries. He'd show me chords on the old Cass guitar. He was the damnedest player I'd seen, though I hadn't seen much. I was a kid. I wondered why my daddy wasn't famous, playing guitar like he did. I asked him. He looked funny at me. It was like he was an outlaw and I'd asked why he wasn't locked up. He never did answer, except in his way. He was smoking cigarettes one night. He blew rings and I thought they were the coolest things. "Know what those are?" he said. "Those are nooses."

I take a drink, a drag. I say to Delia, "So anyway, my daddy went on like always. He got gone."

After those few days of bedroom bliss and front-porch musing, my daddy would get itchy. Night would fall and the road would call to him. He'd take off. South, usually. Memphis in particular had him on a string. Then, one summer, a song he'd recorded for some old record label was done up by this young band. It was souped-up, sounded old and new all at once. It was slick and raw at the same time, had a good coating of river muck and moon dust both upon it. It was a hit and the record label got the idea they'd find ol' John Gaunt and cut a record with him, too. They'd soup him up, make him sound old and new all at once. They'd slick up his rawness.

I tell Delia all this and she says, "Well, damn those record company bastards for wanting to find your daddy and put him in a clean suit of clothes and prop him up on a stage and put a li'l something in his pockets besides his hands."

"Well, yeah," I say. "But he went along with it. For a while, he did. So songs were cut and a tour was set. There was a little jet. My daddy would be traveling with this young band, you see. He'd open for them."

"Oh, fuck." It's the first thing I've heard Delia say that I'd file under *heartfelt*.

"No, it didn't crash. The little jet went up and came down. Smooth landing. But my daddy wasn't on it. Maybe he was scared to fly. Maybe it was that simple. But I think that smooth landing was what scared him—the smooth landing, and then all that attention he'd be getting, that dead-on shot he could finally take at fame. So he just—"

"Disappeared?"

"Something like that. He was on the verge. It was his version of his daddy's Sun Records moment. And like he used to say, something happened. I don't know what. My daddy more or less just drifted away, and I can't say there was much surprise in that.

I thought—I'm sure my ma thought—that in the end he'd come home one less time than he left."

"Is he alive?" Delia doesn't seem to think John Gaunt had enough natural ambition to sustain life.

"I don't know."

7

Malcolm drove and Souse rode shotgun. About two in the morning, they stopped for coffee outside a little Pennsylvania town. Souse, recounting the tale, couldn't recall the little town's name. In my mind, I called it Sepia.

There was a roadside diner. They took their coffee outside in paper cups and drank it sitting on the bumper while beautiful Sara Power lay sleeping in the backseat.

"You figure out how we're going to steal a guitar from that factory, Malc?" Souse said.

"I thought you were the brains of this operation, Souse."

"That's just some shit you said, Malcolm. We both know that."

"Yeah." Malcolm smiled. Being nailed to the wall tickled only a bit. He said, "I figure I'll do the stealing, Souse. You just stay outside and keep watch. You and Sara can do that. As for the plan, I was leaning toward getting in and getting out."

"Well, good. I thought you might just have to wing it."

"I figure getting in is the only hard part. There'll be some back door to jimmy, probably."

"Jimmy," Souse said. "You talk like a real outlaw."

"I'd rather not bust a window."

"I'd rather you not."

"Then, once I'm inside, well . . . ," Malcolm said. "I'll listen to see if one calls out to me. She'll start playing all by her lonesome and I'll know."

"Are all guitars women, Malcolm Gaunt?"

"If they're not, that's a damn-sure waste of good curves."

They sat on the car bumper in the black Pennsylvania night. They drank their coffee. They breathed in night air and coffee steam.

"You worried?"

"Worried?" Souse wondered how a man of sensible stock could be anything other than worried. "Nah," he said.

"Or anyway, not so you'd want to let Sara Power know."

"Why you say that?"

"You're sweet on her."

"Nah, I just like looking at her."

"That's your problem, Souse Milton. You just look. You got to grab sometimes."

"Maybe she doesn't want to be grabbed."

"Girl like that can't be gotten any other way. But hold on tight, would be my advisement."

"You have designs on her yourself."

"Designs." Malcolm said the word like it was a toy, child's play. "I kind of do like her. Admittedly, admittedly. She's got fight, along with her other charms. And she wants nothing more than to show the fair city of Scranton her fine backside. We could go places, me and a girl like that. We could do things."

"Well, then."

"I'm just saying."

"We best get going."

"Yeah, got guitars to steal and all. We could get you one, you know. We could be a band. We could find some drum factory on the way home, if beating sticks is more your thing. I make you for more of a listener, though."

"Yepper, that's me," Souse said. "I'll just play the jukebox. I'll play your records, when you get famous enough to make some. That'll do me. I'm going to own my daddy's bar someday. That's my stake in the world."

"You want nothing more than to pour the fair city of Scranton a cold one."

"Well."

"That's why you and her, you know . . . It just, I don't know, wouldn't work."

"You say. Says you."

"Tell you what, Souse. Take your best shot. I'll stand back. I got my mind set on going south once I get that guitar, anyway. Memphis, I think. That's a town where things are going to bust. But I don't necessarily need to take a woman with me, see. I can get one when I get there, from what I hear of Memphis."

"You don't think she's one in a million?"

"Oh, sure. She is that. But you know, Souse, there's other millions out there."

"So Memphis, huh?"

"Got my mind set on it, yeah."

"That guitar'll take you there, huh?"

"Yeah."

"Well, we'd better go and get it."

The car door creaked and Sara stepped out. She was a little

bit woozy at this late hour. She leaned against the car, her hair a lovely mess, eyes half-shuttered. She said, "Where are we, boys, besides not there yet?"

"Hey, honey babe," Malcolm said. "We just stopped for coffee. Fuel, you know. I'm going back inside to get me a refill and then we'll be back on the road like stripes, sure enough."

Sara yawned. "Well, go on, then," she said.

Malcolm stood up, then leaned down to Souse.

"Here's your shot, Souse. Just you and her. Don't be sweet and don't have designs. She ain't that kind of girl. She ain't a girl at all. She went clear to woman some years ago. Go and grab her. Win her the old-fashioned way. Play dirty—tell the truth. Tell her I'm a no-account musician who will break her heart. Because like as not, I will."

Souse watched Malcolm stride into the diner, settle at the counter, and hail a blond waitress with a wag of a cigarette. He saw the waitress's smiling eyes and her shaking head.

"Calling her honey babe, you can bet," Sara Power said. "And her thinking she's the only one for miles."

Souse walked over to Sara. He offered her a cigarette and lit it. They stood leaning against the car, Souse sorting through a line of talk for something to say. Two minutes, three. Nothing. They just stood watching Malcolm work that waitress.

"You don't have to say anything," Sara said. "I know."

"Well."

Another minute, two. Now Malcolm came out the diner door.

"You ready, honey babe? And how about you, Souse, you rascal, you?"

"Old rake."

"Now that we all got names like proper bad folk, let's go steal us that guitar."

~ ~ ~

Delia drifts to sleep and I strum the old guitar. I'm writing the next song the world won't hear. I'm writing it on a bar napkin from a Texas dive called the Midnight Shift. I sing the words as they come to me:

> *Crucifix*
> *Guitar picks*
> *and Buddy Holly's glasses*
> *Pray God save our souls*
> *Pray God cover our asses*

~ ~ ~

Malcolm parked the Pontiac across the street from the guitar factory. He cut the engine. "All righty, then," he said, and stepped outside onto the sidewalk. He stretched and settled his bones from the four-hour drive. He stepped into the moonshine and took a look at himself, dressed all in black to match that night and those eyes dark as notes on sheet music.

"He was some stuff," Souse Milton said to me, sitting in the empty bar that bore his name and his daddy's, sipping whiskey. Summer was about shot and the jukebox was on a Johnny Cash jag. It played "Cry! Cry! Cry!" and "Train of Love" and the one where Johnny wonders if he'll ever be able to forget his baby. Souse stopped talking when that one played. He stopped drinking, even.

Then the song ended, and silence. When Johnny took to singing "Get Rhythm" or some such, Souse took up again with the story.

"Sara started to stir," Souse said. "She sat up and sighed. She pushed that wild hair from her eyes. She sat watching him. He looked, I don't know, like a movie star or something. That's how he seemed to me. I could only imagine how he seemed to Sara. So I watched her watching him. He lit a cigarette and smoked it and cocked his head. It's like he felt like that movie star, like a character up there on the screen. And she just watched him. I knew then, you know."

"Knew what, Souse?"

"That I'd lost any shot at the damnedest woman ever was."

I borrowed a word from Souse. I wanted to say more, but no more would come, no more would do. I wanted to say it was all right, that he was a good man, a better man. I wanted to say, *Goddamn those Gaunts, anyway.* I just said, "Well."

Souse looked at me. It seemed to be a look of astonishment, beamed across five decades. "And you know, I was all right with that," the old bartender said. "You lose a girl to a movie star sometime, Luther, and see how it feels. It's not so bad, really. It's not really such a distant second to getting the girl. Because you know you couldn't have held onto a girl like that. Because losing a girl to a movie star is almost worth bragging about. It makes a good story, anyway. So I was all right with that. And yet . . ."

Souse perked an ear. The jukebox was between songs. A couple walked in, took the table up front. The man hailed Souse, said, "Two short glasses, good man." Souse poured and I delivered. They were a good-looking couple, couldn't keep their eyes off each other. They didn't even seem to notice I'd come and gone.

"Young and in love," Souse said when I joined him back at the bar. "That's what you need to be, instead of sitting here drinking with an old man, listening to his stories. You got a girl you're sweet on, Luther Gaunt?"

"Nah, not really," I said. It wasn't even much of a lie. "I'm where I want to be just now. I want to hear the stories first. I want to know what I'm up against, being a Gaunt in this world. I want to know the full history of my nature. I want to know all I can—why my daddy and his were the way they were. I want to know if there's any free will in there, any wiggle room. I want to know if I can be—don't laugh—a Gaunt and a good man both."

Souse Milton didn't laugh. He only smiled. He threw an arm around me and said, "So there's not so much at stake for you, is there? Only everything."

"I guess you could say."

"Well. I ought to get back to the story then. Where was I?"

"You and Sara Power, you were sitting in that Pontiac, watching that movie star Malcolm Gaunt. He was smoking a cigarette with his head cocked, looking cool. I believe you said it was that moment when you realized it."

"Except I was wrong," Souse said. "I wasn't near so lucky. See, I'd overestimated Malcolm in one way and underestimated him in another. You'll see that, in time. As for Sara, well, she was way beyond my powers. But I didn't know that then either. Back then, I was just watching her watching him, thinking I knew it all."

Malcolm smoked the cigarette down to almost nothing and flicked it onto the curb. "All righty, then," he said again.

Sara said, "So what's your plan, rake?"

"I'm going to get inside that factory some way and walk among those guitars," he said. "I'll find some that are finished and I'll listen for what one calls out to me. I'll go to her. I'll put my ear to the sound hole. I'll run a hand up and down her neck, a finger down and around her curves."

"Will you two do it there on the factory floor," Sara said, "or will you need to be getting a room on the way home?"

"Now honey babe," he said, smiling.

She said, "Don't honey babe me," but she was smiling, too.

Malcolm went to fetch the empty guitar case from the trunk. Souse met him there, said, "Let me get that."

He figured he'd best insinuate himself into the heist. If he couldn't be a real outlaw, he'd at least be roadie to one. He'd already lost the girl, but there was still the matter of pride and finishing as strong a second as possible. He was a sensible man, but he was a man, still.

"Nah, but thanks. I got it, Souse."

"Malcolm, let me get that."

He reached for the handle, but Malcolm turned with the case and set out across the parking lot. Souse followed and then stepped in front of him.

"We talked about this, remember?" Malcolm said. "I was going after that guitar and you were staying out here with Sara."

"I know, but . . ." Souse stopped, and then, "You could have humiliated me at home, you know. You could have done it at the bar with all the boys watching. I'd at least have gotten a full night's sleep in my own empty bed. You didn't have to bring me all the way to Jersey City and steal a guitar just to win her from me."

"Souse, listen. It's not like that."

"Goddamn you, Malcolm Gaunt."

"Goddamn me all you want, but listen. Here's how this is going to happen. I'm going inside that factory and steal a guitar. You're going to stay out here and—"

"And what? Watch her pine for you?"

"That girl don't pine. She ain't got it in her to pine."

"You want her, though."

"I want a lot of things, Souse."

"You're damn good at getting them."

This gave Malcolm pause. It was something he'd thought about himself. He said, "You say it like it's my greatest fault. I won't say it's not."

Then Malcolm set out across the empty front lot toward the factory, a man in black with his empty guitar case in one hand. He was about to disappear around the corner when Sara shouted to him. He stopped and turned.

"I know all guitars are women!" she said. "I just wonder, are all of them whores, too?"

Malcolm just smiled.

After a stretch of silence in the muddy-brown Merc, Delia says, "So how'd you get the old guitar?"

"Well, that's the other thing. It came one day in a box in the mail with a Memphis postmark. That was about five years ago. There was a note, but it didn't solve any mysteries. It said,

> *Luther,*
>
> > *This is for you, son. It's the one thing I can give you. I'm sorry I haven't given you more. Treat her right and she'll give you songs.*
>
> *Love,*
>
> *John Gaunt,*
> *Chip-off-the-ol'-block son of Malcolm, wayward father of Luther, sorry-bastard husband of Molly*

"The note was in an envelope from a motel called the Getwell Inn. It's in Memphis. Or it was. I tried to call, but it was long gone. But I had Cassie. I had that old Special Rider guitar with all those songs inside. The old ones my daddy's daddy, Malcolm Gaunt, would sing, and the less-old ones my daddy, John Gaunt, would sing, and the new ones I found myself, heard myself, singing. We lived in a row house in our little gray city of the North. I'd sit on the stoop out front and play the old guitar. A girl would come around. Her name was—"

"But enough about her," Delia says. "Unless it ended poorly, and then maybe."

"Like how she did nothing but tease me and I left her for a Patsy Cline album cover?"

Delia laughs and says, "The songs. Tell about the songs. Tell about Cassie putting out."

I grab a pack of smokes from the dash and shake out two. I hand one back to Delia and she leans in to take it. It lounges on those ruby-red, painted-up lips. I flick the cigarette lighter, but suddenly I'm not so steady of hand. Delia steadies my hand with hers and leans in close to light her cigarette, then leans in closer still to light mine. My strumming hand is warm with the cigarette lighter and Delia's touch; it's the heat I sometimes feel when playing.

8

"Your grandfather, he disappeared around the corner of that factory building. We watched him go. We listened. He was whistling. It was a bluesy tune. I liked it. We could hear it and then we couldn't and then we were alone. We leaned against that Pontiac. There wasn't a sound at all. Not even crickets. It was like they'd disappeared around the corner with him, trying to learn that song he was whistling. So that left just the two of us, and all that silence."

"It's hard to know what to say sometimes," I said. "All these words are running through your head, but they get jumbled. It's hard."

"Sometimes a drink helps."

"Sometimes a drink does," I said. "Would have been nice, I guess, if there was a bottle handy that night in Jersey City."

"Well, in fact, there was. It was under the front seat. A bottle of wine. It was cheap stuff, but it was wine, all right. So we passed the bottle and drank and smoked cigarettes and had a little party there. After a bit, he finally began to talk, say things."

I was sitting on the front porch of my grandmother Sara's house. She'd taken up the story, finally. I was older by then. Old enough, I guess. Or anyway, she said it was time I knew.

They sat on the curb that long-ago New Jersey night, that wine bottle between them. He lit her cigarette and watched her smoke it.

"Sara," Souse finally said, "you know I like a good ruckus."

"Yes?"

"It's just that . . ."

"What is it, Henry?"

He hadn't been called that since he was a boy, but it was his name. It was his daddy's name.

"It's just that . . . I don't need to be the one who makes it."

"Henry."

"Yes, Sara?"

"Sensible Henry Milton."

"Yes, well."

"I'm not saying that's such a bad thing, but . . ."

"He'll do you wrong, Sara." He had just enough wine and courage in him now. "He'll be out the door first chance, heading south or somewhere."

"He'll take me with him. We'll go together."

"The three of you."

"If I can't win out over a box of pine, I'll go home and stay."

"I don't think they're made of pine. You're thinking of a casket. Guitars are made of . . . I don't know. Birch or something."

Souse laughed for no reason but that he'd had enough wine to laugh. He ran a hand across Sara's cheek. It felt warm. He leaned in and kissed her there. She turned to him then, full lips.

Then they were in the backseat of the Pontiac.

I'm telling Delia the story. I wonder if she's still listening. I doubt it. But then she says, "I don't know if it was mercy or love or the wine, how they ended up in the backseat. But I know one thing."

"What's that, Delia?"

"I know how this one ends."

They were standing outside the car, after. They were down to no wine and one cigarette. He lit it for her.

"You're going to choose him, aren't you?" He didn't know how he knew.

"Yes."

"Why, Sara?"

"This is for me," she said, watching Malcolm walk toward them, guitar case in hand.

"And that?" Souse Milton said, motioning to the backseat.

"That was for you, Henry," she said. "And I'm afraid it'll have to last you."

Malcolm took out the guitar and set down the case. He held the guitar by the neck and then he hitched it up, cradled the thing. He looked down at it, that Cassandra Special Rider the color of whiskey and water.

He played a lick. He let that swiped guitar ring out. He seemed about to break into a train song or blue yodel. But then he stopped and checked his watch. "Uh-oh. Got to hit it, young lovers," he said. "I may have stolen a guitar, but I only borrowed this car."

Delia considers the story. She asks if there's an upshot to it.

"A moral, you mean?"

"No, Luther, an upshot. I'm not trying to learn any lesson

here. That's for you. I just want to know all that happened, the fallout—who went to jail and who went home and who ended up alone, all that."

"Well, yeah, Delia, there's a bit of that. My grandma Sara Gaunt told it to me. And old Souse Milton said, yeah, that's pretty much how it was. They both even managed to smile about it. What happened was, there was a big fight."

Souse took out after Malcolm. He threw wild roundhouses, kicked and cursed. It was the wine doing the cursing and the hurt doing the kicking. The roundhouses he must have picked up from one of Joe Louis's doomed challengers.

They had themselves a good scrap without Malcolm even doing much fighting. He managed to set aside his newly beloved—Cassandra was her name—and then mostly tried to protect himself.

"Police showed up," I say.

"And so they arrested Souse, I reckon for fighting," Delia says, "and Malcolm for grand theft guitar."

"You'd think, but no." I smile. "Turns out Malcolm didn't steal that guitar. He ordered it from that dry-goods store back in Scranton and was making payments on it. He ordered it out of that catalog. The theft was just this scheme he'd dreamed up to—"

"To make himself seem dangerous. Career move, like the old bluesman saying he sold his soul to the devil down at the crossroads."

"No," I say. "It was something else. Sara reckoned it and Souse said it was fact. Malcolm had dreamed up this whole scheme to get Souse and Sara alone, far from home, to see if maybe his buddy could summon up his nerve and some secondhand gumption."

"He wanted Sara and Souse to be together, huh? I hadn't figured Malcolm for a romantic." She says that last word, *romantic*, as if it's a medical condition for which nothing can be done but staging telethons and praying to the saints.

"Well, that's about what Souse said to Malcolm. And Malcolm said what he'd said before. He said he liked her, loved her, but hell, he could always fall for some new woman down in Memphis when he got there."

"So Malcolm Gaunt was a scoundrel," Delia says, "but an honest one. I see."

The cops sorted through the situation. Malcolm had the paperwork for the guitar. He produced it with a sheepishness that Sara found attractive. The cops were going to haul them off for disturbing the public. But hell, there wasn't any public around to disturb. It was Factoryland. And Malcolm was sober, so he could drive. And the cops couldn't take their eyes off Sara. They hadn't seen her like.

"So they just let them all go," I say, finishing the story. "Wrote the whole thing off to two guys scrapping over a girl."

"America's pastime," Delia says.

I sigh. I say, "So Malcolm drove and Sara rode shotgun. Sensible Henry Milton stretched out in the back, sleeping off all that wine."

A month after the heist that wasn't, Malcolm Gaunt married Sara Power. Souse Milton was best man. It was the Fourth of July, 1939.

PART II

Goners

1

A song called him south that last time. The song said, "Go to Eula." Where she could be found, the song had not said and Malcolm did not know. But the song was in his head; his lungs sounded it and his ears perked and heard it and his bones took limber heed. He strummed on. The song passed to the strings of the old guitar and to the morning breeze and the morning breeze sang it back.

This is the old family story, the one they told themselves and then told me. I added some chords that feel right, notes that ring true to me.

"Go to Eula," the song said, "go now."

There was not a Eula in his life. There never had been. It was an old, Southern-sounding name and so he made for Memphis, the capital of a certain patch of the South, the kingdom of song. This was 1953, and Sam Phillips down at Sun was said to be looking for that white man who could sing black.

Malcolm figured maybe Eula was in Memphis, too. It set him to wondering: Was she a looker? Would he know her when he saw her? Maybe Eula dipped snuff and cussed a blue streak. Maybe Eula already had a man. Or men.

The song had not said. The songs were that way sometimes. The songs were gods to the Gaunts and spoke in godlike, mysterious ways.

"Go to Eula, go now."

I'm telling Delia the story the way I've pieced it together from all the sources—from my daddy and my grandmother, from Souse, from the letters I found, the newspaper clippings. Some of it just appears in my head, those gods speaking to me as they spoke to Malcolm.

"So he made for Memphis," I say, the story like an old record that spins and spins, keeps coming around again. "He made it by foot and by hitching and finally by train. He stood—"

"Wait, back up," Delia says. "What about Sara?"

So I tell her.

The first couple of years were good. Wildness held sway over the land and fireworks lit the night sky. Sara would go out with Malcolm on his jaunts. He called them jaunts, as if they were some little stretch of the legs you could walk back from. Some were one-nighters and sometimes they'd stay gone for weeks. Malcolm would play and Sara would count the money. She had a way with bar owners. No one shorted the Malcolm Gaunt Medicine Show. The money was good, for mere guitar slinging. They traveled light. They'd hole up in roadside motels, the three of them in bed together, Malcolm strumming Cassie's strings and singing songs of Sara.

Sara was flesh and bone and rushing blood. She was wild curls and wicked curves. She was muse to the man, art to the artist. She had nothing to fear from a box of . . . what was it? Pine? No, birch.

Or so she thought, and rolled over onto him; she took the guitar by the neck and let it drop to the floor.

But later, hours after, she'd stir in the night and he'd be across the room holding the guitar, not even strumming it, just listening for what it might say to him: sweet talk and come-ons, secret chords, mystery tunings.

"Come to bed, Malcolm."

"I will directly."

"It's the middle of the damn night." ·

"Shh, now, honey babe."

"What pet name do you have for her?"

"She doesn't answer to me. It's the other way around."

"That doesn't sound like you."

"I'm going for a walk."

"You want company?"

"Got company already."

"What say you come back to bed and I break that guitar over something hard?"

"You got anything particular in mind?" He couldn't help but smile then. He set the guitar on the chair and came to bed.

"Yeah, I figured her a match for Malcolm, him being just a man, after all," Delia says.

"But it wasn't Malcolm she was up against," I say. "Not really. It was Cassie, and she may have been the one female in the world Sara couldn't beat. Cassie was a guitar and so she was . . ."

"What, little Luther Gaunt? Tell me." Delia has her chin on the back of the front seat. She has dope and grape pop on her breath. I don't know where she came by either. "No, don't. Because I know already."

"She was perfect," I say. "Cassie was all curves and songs and didn't even know there was a woman named Sara. So it wasn't even close to a fair fight, because it wasn't even close to a fight."

"It's still just a box of pine." She's playing with me.

"Birch," I say. "It's got to be the right wood."

She stretches an arm over the front seat, rests it on my right shoulder. "That's right, I forgot," she says. "I must have fallen asleep in shop class or something."

A fight would have sustained Sara. So she tried for one. She tried to take it out on Malcolm. She blackened his eye one night in the hills of Kentucky. I know this for certain because there's a picture of my granddaddy's shiner. It looks like he took the picture himself. It's a close-up shot, blurry. But it was a pretty good pop she gave that handsome Gaunt face. On the back of the picture was written, in Sara's hand,

Christmas Day 1940. Morehead, Ky. Worst Christmas ever. We exchanged gifts. I didn't think much of mine, but Malcolm wore his for a few days after.

I tell Delia that part.

"What did Malcolm give Sara?" she says. "I don't reckon he popped her one back."

"I don't guess he did. He wouldn't have. I don't think he'd have turned the other eye, though. I suspect he took Cassie and made for those Kentucky hills, before she got busted up to splinters."

"Cass. Cassie. Jesus, Luther. Y'all got to stop talking about that box of pine—"

"Birch."

"—like it's a living, breathing, humping, bitching, moaning, slinking, ass-shaking, tits-in-a-T-shirt *she*." Delia wraps her arm around my neck—whether affection or choke hold, it's difficult to say.

"Anyway," I say, "Sara had figured it out by now. First she'd thought she was in a fight she couldn't lose and then she'd thought she was in a fight she couldn't win. But now she knew there wasn't any fight to fight. It was then, I guess, she realized the thing about the road."

It just keeps spooling out. There's no getting to the end of it. The days take the names of towns and cities that are all the same, only different. The nights take the names of dive bars and junk motels. And Sara was just one more woman watching Malcolm, one more who'd never really have him as long as that Cassandra Special Rider guitar was, like Delia said, putting out.

Delia loosens her grip, gives me a slow pat on the cheek. She runs a couple of fingers across my mouth, slips a finger in.

"Hey, Jimmy Lee," I say—slur, really.

Jimmy Lee sleeps on. Jimmy Lee would have slept through Altamont.

Delia lies back in the backseat. Grape and dope fumes linger faint in her wake.

I don't say anything for the longest time, and then, "So Sara told herself she didn't want him. That sustained her through the balance of Kentucky. It's not such a big state, going north to south. But down in Nashville, the deepest south she ever got, she made straight for the train station. She made for home, left Cassie to Malcolm."

Malcolm made it a home a couple of months later. He reeked of the road and its splendors. He was tired but had a new batch of songs. He sat on the porch of the small house in the evenings of the next few weeks and played them.

Sara asked if he was done with the road.

"Now honey babe."

"Don't honey babe me."

He picked at the guitar, played a bluesy note and then another—a string of them, a procession.

"You could get a regular gig playing at Souse's. You could be king of Scranton."

Malcolm went out that night for a pack of cigarettes. He was gone three months that time—not that she was counting by then.

Sara Gaunt died the summer I turned seventeen. It was then I found the letters. They were in a shoebox on a high shelf in the same closet where I'd found the old records. There was one from Malcolm to her that read,

> *You can hate me, Sara. You ought to. Some mornings, I'm not so crazy about me myself. But night comes around and so do I. That's just how it is with me. I haven't been true to you, but I never lied to you, Sara. I never said I'd change. I never meant to. You could have married a better man, but you didn't want him. He was standing right there. You had the choice between good sense and a bad penny. I'm a bad penny still. But I keep rolling. That's what bad pennies do, in my experience. We can't buy anything of value and we don't shine like your better denominations, but Lord, we roll just fine. It's Nashville tonight. I'm playing this lounge on the edge of downtown. I could use you here, the way you had, that look. The manager, see, he doesn't seem to want to pay me what I earned. He thinks a bad penny wouldn't know what to do with actual paper folding money, I guess. But I met a fellow here who says there's a record producer over in Memphis, man named Sam*

Phillips. He's supposed to be looking for a white man with the Negro sound and the Negro feel. He says he could make a billion bucks with that man, way I heard it. I don't know how many bad pennies that is, but, my old honey babe, it's a lot.

There was another letter, dated a week later. It was post-marked Jackson, Tennessee:

Met this guy named Carl, didn't catch his second name, but plays even better guitar than me. Damn. He cut me pretty bad. But I'm better looking, you know. He asked did I hear about that record producer Sam Phillips, looking for the white man with the Negro sound and the Negro feel. I said I heard that was just some made-up tale.

And there was a note that Sara wrote but never sent:

People talk about having it to do all over again and what they'd do different. But that's a lie and I won't bother telling it. I can't. I'll just say this one thing. I'm sorry, Henry.

2

S o now it was 1953. Malcolm set out for Memphis, that last time, by walking and then by hitching. He'd stop and play in the towns and cities and people would listen. Some would throw bills and change into his open guitar case. One day, he looked up and saw a train station before he saw another bar, and so . . .

Two days later, he stood outside the Memphis station, tired and worn, bones sore from the ride like hard-ridden rails, the guitar case at his side. He let his arms drop to his sides, let his fingers dangle, those fingers long and thin like the fringe on some old cowboy singer's stage shirt.

He looked about, for to see Eula when she appeared. He had no doubt she would. He smiled at the sight of Memphis, his old friend. Memphis never failed to deliver on women, was his experience. He raised a cigarette to his lips and let it rest there, unlit, for the longest time. He thought, *Eula, Eula. What rhymes with Eula?*

Malcolm was a traveled man pushing forty, but with vast talents and that handsome mug. He stood outside that train station watching the women, thinking of how they wore their bodies, how they moved in them. Eula would sway, was Malcolm's guess, as if new to the city and shaking off country dust.

> *Eula, my Eula*
> *my flicker, my flame*
> *Eula, my Eula*
> *my wildness you tame*

A tallish woman clipped by, all city, no country dust on this one. She had harsh eyes and harsh hair, wore her body like first frost. Malcolm felt a chill even on this summer day and lit his cigarette for warmth. He stepped forward for a better view of the street beyond.

> *Eula, my Eula*
> *forever by your side*
> *Eula, my Eula*
> *'til death do I die*

He unsnapped his guitar case and hitched up his guitar. He strummed and he sang. He sang the song of Eula, closed his eyes and saw her, opened them and there she was: about guitar-high to Malcolm Gaunt, with a man's white shirt over her wide sweep of hips, a camera slung around her neck. She had short hair bleached blond and blue jeans, black shoes with a heel, black shades over her eyes.

"Eula?"

"You buying?"

3

They walked across the street and into the Arcade Restaurant, loud with the song of bustle and the breakfast crowd. There was an open booth for two on the far side and there they sat and ordered coffee, black, and were served it by a tall, thin girl with yellow movie-star hair.

"Pretty girl, you think?" Eula said after the waitress had spun off with their order. "Long and tall, like y'all men like?"

"Could do with some gravy on her bones, would be my personal observation."

"You like gravy, do you?"

"Why, I'm partial to all the fixings," Malcolm said.

Eula leaned across the table and sang low to him, a song about a big, fat mama. "That's one by Little Junior Parker and his Blue Flames. It's gonna be out on Sun Records, but it ain't yet. I've heard it, but I can't tell you where. You heard its like?"

"Can't say as I have. Is it a slow blues?"

"Nah, man. It starts with these guitar licks got steam coming off. Then it chugs and goes. It sounds a little country, but I don't mean all slow and whiny like Hank Williams. Hank's dead and buried and this is something new coming."

"God rest his soul," Malcolm said. "Hank."

"That be the rest with the *w* on the front end?" Eula smiled.

"Aren't you the smart one."

"Pride of Humes High."

"I thought they'd have taught you better respect for your American heroes there."

"Ah, praise be to ol' Hank. I grew up listening to his stuff. My daddy played it all the damn time. I like a little country whine, myself. I'm just telling you there's something new coming. Something wilder and faster. I can just feel it. I feel it in my feet and on up into my knees and thighs. It makes my feet stomp through my shoes and it makes my knees knock through my skin. I can't even begin to tell you, Malcolm Gaunt, what it does to my thighs."

Eula sipped her coffee and Malcolm thought he'd say something while she did. He didn't know what in hell it would have been. But anyway, she beat him to it. She said, "I don't know what all kind of music you play, just from that little bit at the train station. But I'm telling you this on account of I like the look of you— on account of I like an older man, a seasoned one. So listen, you: There's a fast train coming—fast like the Choctaw Rocket—and you can hop on board or you can watch it bust on by. Don't matter. It's coming but ain't stopping."

"How you know these things, girl?"

"Told you. I just know. That, and I heard it said. Sam Phillips at Sun Records told me. Well, he said it to somebody else and I heard it. We were having lunch, but not together. I was in the next booth, listening."

"Did he say something about wanting to find a white man could sing Negro? Did he say he could make a billion bucks off such a man?"

"He may of."

"That Little Junior Parker you mentioned."

"Yeah?"

"He white?"

"He's the coffee," Eula said, "ain't the cream."

"So, then, Sam Phillips, he's still looking for his white man?"

"You'd have to ask Sam that. I could show you his place and where he eats his lunch. You want to make a billion bucks, Malcolm Gaunt?"

Malcolm thought about this.

"Hell, I ain't in it for the money. I'm a musician, pure as can be. I'm in it for the women."

Malcolm and Eula laughed and barely noticed the yellow-haired girl had come by with the food. They couldn't remember ordering it, even. They just found themselves eating, eggs over light and bacon crisp, biscuits and sausage gravy. She made him look outside, at some corner commotion, and then stole a piece of bacon from his plate; their hands brushed as she made off with it and he let her.

"So what kind of music you play, Malcolm Gaunt?" Eula said.

"Guess."

"Old poky country with a shot of blues, I reckon," she said. "And I reckon you play it good, too, and that the women, they like it. Reckon I would, too. But you're not a young man. Handsome, yeah. But not young. You up to hopping on that train that's coming but ain't stopping, Malcolm Gaunt?"

Well, he thought. "Well," he said.

Malcolm just smiled at her then, watched her wear that

body of hers like it was a dress she might be about to shed. She had a whole lot of body and not much of height, looked like she just walked out of some blues song. He smiled and watched her through the haze of coffee steam and well-shook country dust.

"Well, nothing," she said, her voice going low. "Hank's dead and you standing there with a shovel in your hand won't change it. It's time for something new. You got to listen to this other record by Little Junior and those Blue Flames of his. Let's us go to my place and I'll play it for you."

"Well," he said again.

"And that guitar," she said. "It's a beaut, but what's it, twenty years old? You need to get you an electric."

They finished eating and Malcolm paid and so now they stood outside the Arcade. He leaned against a light pole, pulled the guitar from the case, and hitched up the thing. He played her a song. It was Bill Monroe's "Blue Moon of Kentucky," as yet untouched by the Boy Who Would Be King. Elvis Presley was fresh out of Humes High, looking for steady work after that temp job at the machine shop ran out.

He played it teardrop slow. Eula stood watching, tapping her high-heeled shoe, but ahead of the beat, impatient. "I like what you do with those long fingers—I'm even beginning to wonder what else they might be good for—but Lord, Malcolm Gaunt. Put that foot on the gas. You got the gift, man. But *go!*"

Flatter the man's guitar playing, flatter the man. So Malcolm gave it a run. He revved it up to a full sprint, a good country rip. But Eula just said, "No, harder, Malcolm Gaunt. Harder." And he did.

4

They walked from downtown toward where she lived. They walked a long way. She had youthful energy and he had long strides. They headed north on Main and turned east at Union, put their backs to the big river. They stopped at The Peabody hotel and there Malcolm bought a newspaper. He turned the pages as they walked, checked the headlines and ads without expectation that either would put the touch on his ever-charmed life. "Victory Under Christ—Rector Points Path." He thought of the old Scranton newspaperman, talking in headlines. Veal loin chops, $0.29 a pound. Ladies' Scuffies, zipper tops, sponge rubber soles, $1.69. GE was touting a new clock radio for $28.95.

" 'Why be alarmed?' " Malcolm said, reading of the latter item, " 'Wake up to music.' "

They were standing at the 700 block of Union Avenue. Malcolm didn't know why they'd stopped, but it was a damn sight easier to read the Memphis newspaper standing still.

"Why the hell I need a $30 alarm clock that sings to me in the morning when I got a guitar-playing man already?" Eula said. "And anyway, sometimes it takes more than a song to get me rolling in the morning."

Malcolm turned the page and looked at the Rainey Drug Store ad in lieu of answering so bold and forward of a woman. He saw a "cowboy gee-tar" at a buck forty-nine and showed it to her and smiled. He laughed. She laughed, too.

He read from the ad. " 'Turn crank,' " he said. " 'It plays.' "

"Been my experience that's how lots of things get going," young Eula said.

Malcolm said only, "Woo-boy," and rolled up the newspaper and stuck it in his back pocket, then said just before he looked up and saw for himself, "So where are we?"

Across the street was Sam Phillips's little storefront recording studio. There was neon in the windows and neon over the door, the latter spelling *S-U-N*, the letters glowing, the color of Mercurochrome, even in the summer daylight.

"Damn hell," Malcolm said. "That's it, huh?"

"It ain't Rainey's Drug Store," she said.

They walked across Union Avenue and to the storefront. Malcolm stood before the door, swaying, as if he needed a nudge. Eula gave him a shove.

"Mr. Phillips in?"

A blond-haired woman looked up from behind the desk in the little front office. She said, "No, he's—"

"Do you know when . . . ?"

She about smiled. There was a desperation to the singers when they appeared at Mr. Sam's door. There was a pleading. *If they could put it into their songs*, she thought, *they'd have something*. She said, "He's on the road for a few days, seeing folks. He'll be back next week. You sing?"

"Sing and play," Malcolm said. He felt like himself, to say the words, felt the old swagger, just standing there in the doorway of the storefront studio that would change the world, once some other, younger man walked in. "Damn straight I do. Um, ma'am."

She smiled. "What do you sound like, Mr., uh . . . ?"

"Malcolm Gaunt, ma'am," he said.

He paused before he answered.

"Negro," he said.

She paused, too, played it cool. She wrote herself a note, as if a white man who had the Negro sound and the Negro feel was something she needed to pick up for Mr. Sam over at Rainey's later that afternoon, along with some aspirin and paper towels.

"Well, all right, then, Mr. . . . . Gaunt, was it? I'll let him know. You playing anywhere around? Mr. Phillips has a man who scouts talent for him."

"Well, sure," Malcolm lied. "My manager's outside. Let me stick my head outside and check."

He stepped outside. "Hey, Eula, baby. Where could I talk myself into a quick gig hereabouts?"

"Sam Phillips want to know?"

"No, the woman."

"That's Marion. She's nice."

"Well?"

"Tell her you're playing the Eagle's Nest in a couple of weeks. Tell her you'll call back with the date."

"I guess I'll be needing a band."

"I know a couple of boys."

"I kind of figured you would."

5

Malcolm wore black pants, a white shirt, a black jacket with white piping, and black shoes, too. He minded not the Memphis heat. He was tall and lanky, had those long, long fingers. There was some gray in his stubble and in his thick head of blackish hair.

He believed in Heaven and he believed in Hell. He believed they were cities on his latest jaunt, same as Tupelo and Montgomery and Hot Springs. He believed a good man's eternal reward would fit in a shot glass without a drop wasted, and that a bad man's pain of damnation could be tempered with a couple of headache powders. He was a Goody's man.

He had that failed marriage back home. This much you know. And he had been shot at four times, hit once—nicked, actually; he was playing at the time and made sure to finish the song. He had spent a month in jail, spread over two decades and four cities. Yeah, those songs from the old Cassandra guitar got him in some stews.

"Thirty-eight," he said when Eula asked his age. They were sitting at Miss Taylor's Restaurant, next door to Sam Phillips's recording studio. They were drinking coffee. Eula had pie.

"Like the gun," she said, waving the fork about like she might have in mind a stickup of Miss Taylor's establishment.

"Well, I wouldn't say a gun. Or anyway, I wouldn't say that one."

"Pistol, ain't it?" Eula leaned forward, let that bleached-blond hair fall over the black shades. She let the shades fall to the end of her button nose. She had brown eyes: big, round chocolate drops. She said, "Oh, yeah, you're a pistol."

He leaned back in the booth, smiled broadly. "Pearl-handled," he said.

She snapped his picture.

"Half-cocked," she said.

His face fell, a mock collapse.

And snapped his picture again.

"I'll make you famous, Malcolm Gaunt."

"By taking my picture? I doubt that."

"Oh, hell no. I'll manage your career. I'll spread the word. It may not be easy with a name like Gaunt. We maybe ought to change it. We could call you the Choctaw Rocket. And you're getting to be on the gray side, so we better hurry. We damn sure better hurry. There's that train that's coming but ain't stopping, the one I told you about. We'll ride it awhile, you and me, and see what happens. We'll get one of those sleeper cars but not sleep."

"You're scandalous, girl," he said.

Flatter the girl's nature, flatter the girl. But she smiled only for a second. She was back to business before her face had the chance to blush. "You know how you played that song, 'Blue

Moon of Kentucky'? Well, did you like it that way? How did it *feel*?"

He thought about this, wondered how to put it, exactly.

"It felt like I was standing on solid ground and then I wasn't. Like the sidewalk was a rug you pulled out from under me. I couldn't feel my fingers. It was like they took to flying. Left my body and went off on their own. That's how it felt. And as for whether I liked it, I don't know. I just don't know, Eula. Or whatever the hell your name is."

He meant to frown now, but he smiled instead. His mind had no say in the matter. He put a hand on her cheek, ran it up through that bleached-blond hair, leaned across that table, and kissed her lips. He thought, *Well, I don't know about changing my name, girl. But I've got more than a notion to change yours.*

"So how old are you, Eula?"

"Twenty-two," she said. "That's a gun, too, but another sort of one."

"Well, then," Malcolm said. "I guess that makes the both of us scandalous."

He paid for the coffee and Eula's pie and they took up walking, east again on Union toward her place.

6

One way to say it is, young Eula knew a lot of men. Another way is, the girl had connections. A couple, three phone calls, and Malcolm Gaunt had a bass player and a drummer and a gig at the Eagle's Nest, out on Lamar Avenue. That gave them the afternoon free for other matters.

"You got a light touch, Malcolm Gaunt," Eula said.

"Why, thank you."

"There are other ways of touching, though. You know what I'm saying?"

"I'm starting to."

Eula stood in the doorway to the kitchen of the small house. This was on a shady Memphis side street. She stood there in the doorway with her whole lot of body and not much of height, wearing that man's white shirt, unbuttoned to show more than just her wide sweep of hips. She had a lit cigarette in one hand and the other hand she ran through the grayish black tangle of Malcolm's hair.

"Damn," she said, "but you're a tall one even on your knees, Malcolm Gaunt."

7

Malcolm sat on the kitchen counter, bent over his guitar, playing low and whispering words that couldn't be heard for the sounds from outside the open window over the sink. There was a screech of tires and wheeze of brakes, a horn's blare, some sort of near-accident, sounded like. He stopped playing but didn't look up.

Eula stood at the sink watching, bare-assed in a man's black jacket with white piping.

He started playing again, his thumb brushing the top strings and his first finger picking the bottom ones. It was a new song— country blues for a bare-assed woman and her guitar-playing man:

> *How far would you go?*
> *I said, how far would you go?*
> *How far would you go, to get gone?*

How far would you go?
Tell me, how far would you go?
How far would you go, to get gone?

A little ways on

His thumb brushed some more and his finger picked. One shuffled and the other loped. The latter doubled back on the former, urged it on, coaxed, pleaded and begged, showed its bare ass and then was gone.

"A little ways on," he sang again, a whisper now. "A little ways on."

Now the loping strings circled around again on the shuffling strings, but the shuffle had broken into a run. There was a chase and the one caught the other and together they hopped a train and rode.

"Holy hell, Malcolm Gaunt," Eula said, dancing bare-assed across the kitchen at him, "that's a billion-dollar sound."

That night, as Malcolm and his new band played the song in the front room, Eula lay in the bedroom in the dark and listened; the walls of the small house shook and shuddered but had not one thing on the girl.

Two weeks later, Sam Phillips's man heard them play at the Eagle's Nest. They played a full set of country and blues all messed up together like Malcolm liked to do, but faster than before—that was Eula's influence, her doing. The girl should have come with a drug warning—she gave off side effects; you couldn't help but feel hopped-up around her, wired. Malcolm was pushing forty but seemed, bounding on that Memphis stage, to be pulling back toward thirty, a gaunt but handsome man with that thick head of black hair, the gray streaks gone now, somehow, and still those eyes dark as notes on sheet music.

After he sang, "A little ways on, a little ways on," he paused and dropped his head, as if existential musings the likes of these were seldom attempted on the Eagle's Nest stage and he had best proceed cautiously. He slow-dragged his left leg across the front of his body. He drummed a thumb on the body of the guitar, then stopped. Silence in the joint. A busboy named Elvis, standing between the stage and the elevated dance floor, stopped and watched like the sky had split before him, revealing all. Then Malcolm moved as if jolted, his black hair blur-swept across his face. He came up banging on the Cassandra Special Rider guitar, singing about heaven and that other place, about the Choctaw Rocket train and Pontiac automobiles, about comings and goings of wayward souls, escapes and retreats, about the gray, besmoked North and the bright, sunny South, about honey babes and wives estranged and Cassie's mighty curves. And he sang of the bare-assed glories of the girl-woman Eula, though by now Malcolm's singing, his song, and his band were so loud, fast, and unhinged that no one could reasonably have said to pick out particular words.

Later, Sam Phillips's man sat on the edge of the stage, shook his head at Malcolm, and said, "Damn, man."

"That a good thing?"

"We'll see."

"Okay, then. Now what?"

"I didn't think I'd ever say this, but . . ."

"But what?"

"Could you tone it down just a little?"

Malcolm grinned at Eula. "I doubt it. But hell, you never do know."

Sam's man handed Malcolm a card. A time and date were written on the back. "Be there," he said, "and we'll see what comes of it."

That night in bed, Malcolm said, "So what'd you think, baby? I don't know, myself. It was all getting a little crazy up there, like it was out of my hands altogether. Like it wasn't me up there anymore. Like it was some other, younger man. Some kid. I kind of wanted to stop and hand the guitar to that busboy standing there, just staring up at me. Say, 'Here, son, you're young. You do this.'" Malcolm was staring at the ceiling, the cracks there. "Me, I like to take things just to the edge, you know. Then I tend to want to look for a nice place to sit and enjoy the view. Have a cool one. Because you get to the edge and then take that next step, you're not in control anymore. There's just a big fall. That's how it felt on stage tonight, like I was falling. I'm not saying it was all bad. It was . . . what's the word? Exhilarating. It was exhilarating as all hell. Lord, it was. God, Eula. But the whole time, my only thought was I knew it would end. I was waiting, the whole time, for some big crash." He meant to pause but found he couldn't stop. "That's some tough shit on a man, is what I'm saying, baby."

And then, "So what'd you think?"

"I liked that dirty shit you sang about me," she said, rolling onto him.

8

"Marry me, Miss Eula," he said.

Malcolm kissed one of her dusty ankles, liked the taste of it.

"Marry the hell out of me."

He savored that dust and flesh and chased them with a drink of beer.

"Marry me at dawn, down by the river, in that dress you wore that one Saturday night."

He leaned back in the brass bed, considered the bottom of his bottle, the last few drinks and dregs. He had the guitar with him, too, and he played a lick.

Eula lay at the opposite end of the bed. She said, "I wasn't wearing a dress."

"Not after a spell, you weren't." He laughed and she did, too. They laughed a lot that year as fall gave way to early winter. They laughed and drank and made that old brass bed sound like what the Boy Who Would Be King conjured the next summer over at Sun Records.

"Well?"

Eula took the old guitar, ran a finger all up and down the neck, then down and around its curves. Eyes closed, she put her lips, her tongue, to one of the silver tuning pegs; she took one, then another, into her mouth. Now with one hand, she strummed the top strings, and the other hand she kept to herself.

That went on for some time, and then she said, with a sidelong look at sated Cassie, "But aren't you already hitched, Malcolm Gaunt?"

She laid the guitar on the floor beside the bed now. She climbed atop Malcolm, shook her head at the man, the bleached-blond hair longer than before and falling more into her big, brown chocolate-drop eyes.

"Well?" he said again.

"You need to be thinking about laying down that song for Sam Phillips."

"Oh, they called. Didn't I tell you? That woman. Marion. She said Sam needed to push it back a few weeks. Reschedule the thing." Malcolm was a pretty fair country liar. He'd made the call; he'd begged the postponement. It was like he'd told Eula after that night at the Eagle's Nest. He liked to come to the edge of crazy and then just kind of cool it. He had his songs from the old guitar and he had a woman wilder than he was, enough scratch in his pocket to buy what drink he wanted; it seemed to him a fool's notion to want to push for the least little bit more. "So I said, 'Well, tell Sam it's his place, not mine.'"

Eula said, "Hmm." Eula said, "Well, that's good. That'll give us some time to, you know, build up the interest. Get you some more shows to play. Spread the word. I'll make handbills to hang from every light pole in Memphis: *Malcolm Gaunt and*

His Billion-Dollar Sound, Live at the Overton Park Shell, Saturday Next. Something like that. And I'm gonna watch you that night from the wings, and then I'm gonna bring you home, if I can tear you away from the girls clawing at you, and then I'm gonna ride you like a gone train. And then, after all that, maybe we can think about me marrying the hell out of you."

"So it's maybe, then."

"Shut up, Malcolm."

"Yes, ma'am."

9

November 1953.

The girl-woman not named Eula got up one morning, put on that man's black jacket with the white piping but didn't button it. She took a long look at herself in the floor-length closet mirror; there was a little more to her whole lot of body and she thought she ought to go and see the doctor so he could tell her what she knew already.

She went to the hairdresser instead, got her hair dyed black.

When she got back home, she said, "I got something to tell you, Malc."

"You got hair black as my jacket."

She lay beside him in the brass bed. The radio was on. It was playing the new one by Little Junior and his Blue Flames. It started with a drum beat like a slow chug. A sax blew a mournful blare. Little Junior sang about a train. And Eula said, "Well, good. With all I got to tell you, I was hoping you'd pick that up on your own."

"I did. I like it. God, you're a whirl of woman, girl." He took her in his arms, let her bury her head against his chest as he kissed that black, black hair.

"My name's not Eula. It's Wanda, which doesn't sound a lick like Eula, so I don't think you can blame ol' Cassie for slurring her words. I think you saw me and took a real hard shine and wanted me to be this Eula. I liked you, too. Still do. So I was willing to be Eula. I never much liked Wanda, as names go. The busboy that first night at the Eagle's Nest, his name's Elvis. I recognized him. He was behind me at Humes. So you can call anybody anything. So I was Eula. I was to you. But the thing, Malc, sweet baby, is that there's another guitar player who knows me as nothing other than Wanda Walls. Walls, that's my married name, see. His name's Frankie, and he's only about three-quarters the man you are—he's a slight, little guy—and just shy of half the musician you are, which still makes him pretty fine, and he shares your fondness for girl-women with a whole lot of body. God love the few of you who do. It's good to see a couple of white men come around to the gospel according to the bluesman. And God, I love you both, but you a little more. I'm not just saying that. I wish I'd known about you before I settled on Frankie. But anyway, there's Frankie. No disputing there's Frankie. He's not so bad. He likes to play that other Little Junior song, the one about the big, fat mama. He's got a smoky voice that sounds real down-low and dirty. He might just have you whipped, Malc, in the vocal department."

" 'Love My Baby,' " Malcolm said. "That's the name of that particular one."

"Yeah, well, and we've had some wedded bliss, all right. But he's a musician and you know how that goes. He's most always gone. I don't know where he is now and I don't know when he'll be back. He usually calls first, but not always. He could be walking up the walk now. Maybe he'll have a wad of cash in his hand to pay the rent, because it's sure as hell due. I get lonely. I have my camera. I take pictures. You know, a hobby. But I look through that camera and see something more than a picture. I see something more than that shiny paper can hold. I see a movie, like. I see action and drama. I'm the director. That's part of why I took my own real hard shine to you. That's why I figured I could be, you know, your manager. But I've settled into being something else. Your Eula. Your woman. Mother of your child, Malc, here in a few months."

Malcolm was up and leaning on one elbow, looking down upon her. He ran a finger through her newly black hair, down between her big, brown, chocolate-drop, crying eyes, to her button nose and lips and on down the length of her body, to the swell there.

He said her name and dabbed at her tears.

10

They were in bed again. They had about worn the damn thing out. It wheezed when it moved a little and it creaked when it moved a little more and it was a full rhythm section when it moved a lot. You could hear it from outside the open bedroom window of the small side-street house whose primary tenant was a musician off playing somewhere, in that musician's way.

"I reckon you got some secrets you haven't told me, too," Eula said.

"Reckon I do."

"A wife back home, probably. Any children?"

"A wife, yes. No kids. There have been some . . . what you call them? Miscarriages."

"What's she like? Do I remind you of her? Is she a handful, too? She have a name?"

Malcolm told it all. He told of Sara and Souse and that night in Jersey City. He told of wedding vows and fireworks, of wander and other lusts. He told of those early days of marriage when Sara would go out with him on the road. He told of those wild curls and guitar curves, her strong will and nature.

"She go to pot? Is that why you're here with me? Because you know—"

"No, it wasn't that. It was other things. She changed in other ways. But I'd go home sometimes—and sometimes to her. Just a few months ago, for a long weekend, we made like old times. We talked and did more than talk. We holed up. I said maybe it was time for me to settle down, be the king of Scranton like she wanted me to be. I called her honey babe, like the old days. I said—"

"The things people say, in weak moments."

"Yeah. They mean them, though."

"But only in those weak moments."

"She knew, too. That was the thing. She knew even if I didn't. So when I felt that itch at the end of that long weekend, I didn't have to scratch and pack, both. My bags were at the front door. She'd packed them already. She knew. I left before dawn. We didn't say anything. I just looked at her, not knowing if she wanted to punch me or cry. There was precedent for the one, and as for the other, well, she was surely due. I turned and walked. Haven't seen her since."

Eula walked naked across the bedroom. She shook the floorboards with her pale heft. She said, "Well, anyway, I'm no threat to her. It's that Cassandra Special Rider guitar. There's never been any secret of that. She's the root of all your evil and she's your salvation, too. I suppose it's gotten to the point of her being more real than me and you and that wife of yours, all of us."

"I don't know about all that."

"We both of us know better. But that's all right by me, Malcolm Gaunt. I'm no pure and innocent thing myself. If I get mine—justice, I mean—I won't go crying about it."

11

Malcolm Gaunt had postponed again with Sam Phillips, but now the day had come for him to appear at Sun Records with his band. It was early yet but seemed a fine day to try and change popular culture for the next half-century.

But then Frankie Walls, a little man as advertised, strode up the walk not with a wad of rent money in his hand but a pistol he called "my trusty." He knew of his woman and her new man. He'd run across a friend of a friend, a drummer in a country band, who had word from Memphis that Wanda, that wife of his, was seen gallivanting—that was the word this drummer used—with another man.

"Gallivanting, you say," Frankie said. He didn't know exactly what that entailed but had his base suspicions.

"Gallivanting," the drummer said, mildly pleased to be able to work that word, one of his personal favorites, into conversation. He was the drummer. He never got to talk. Drummers just kept somebody else's beat. This drummer, he suddenly harbored thoughts of quitting the country band and forming his own outfit called The Gallivanters. He said it again. "Gallivanting, Frankie, is the way I was told it and that's how I'm telling it to you. I don't know the particulars except that I heard this fella was a guitar player, like you. I heard he plays this 1930s Cassandra Special Rider with gold flowers on it. I'm told there's magic between them, this man and his guitar. I heard he has the longest fingers and that he's tall. I heard he's as tall as your Wanda is short. I heard—"

"You hear all that over the thump of your drums?" Frankie said.

The drummer said, "Now Frankie."

This was up in Kentucky, where Frankie had played a country school gymnasium. He was tired from too many nights and too many small towns, but he wasn't of a mind to wait. He could drive back to Memphis and be there before dawn.

He arrived about five, parked two blocks from the side-street house. He strode up the walk.

The bedroom window was open, but the bed was silent. Frankie Walls spun the pistol he called "my trusty" around his trigger finger and thought, *Well, I guess I'm a little late to catch them in the act. Or a little early, one.*

He stepped lightly up the steps, sat leaning against the front of the house just to the side of the bedroom window. He slept in bits and stretches.

Morning broke lazily through the side-street trees. Morning yawned and stretched and set about lolling in the bed of a new day. Frankie had one of those headaches he got, like a crack beginning at the base of his skull and traveling vaguely north up into the back of his head. He raised his head, forced open his eyes. He heard the slight squeak of the bed, then the creak of footsteps upon floor. That would be the man, he figured. Wanda had a whole lot of body, but not that much. He heard the bathroom door open, moments later heard it close.

Then the man was back in bed and Frankie heard whispers of talk he couldn't make out but needn't have. He had some more of those base suspicions. He showed the brightening day his pistol, let a shaft of early-morning sun catch and spread its gleam.

The bed wheezed and then it creaked and then it became that entire rhythm section. He stood listening to the raucous tune and then walked in the house. He didn't concern himself with creeping, such was the noise of the brass bed and that man saying, for reasons unknown to Frankie, "My God, Eula."

12

The Memphis newspaper for that day of '53 said an itinerant musician returned home from the road to catch and shoot and kill his wife and her lover, himself an itinerant musician named Malcolm Gaunt, age thirty-eight, hometown unknown.

It was reported that Frankie Walls shot them dead and then walked out on the porch to await the law. He played the dead man's guitar while he waited. He played some country weepers and then he played a bluegrass tune so fast his fingers took to flying. He was playing a mean Memphis blues called "I'm Gonna Murder My Baby" when the police arrived. His playing was full now of mad flourishes and thudding depths and rippling asides.

The lead officer, who played a little, once upon another lifetime, let Frankie finish the song and then took custody of the guitar.

"A Cassandra Special Rider," the officer said, nodding approval.

"Yeah," said Frankie in his smoky, low voice. "With a woman like that, I don't know what he needed with mine."

The story was just sordid enough to make the front page of the Memphis newspaper. There was an unborn child, cheating spouses, the lower classes on parade. There was, too, the beautiful old Cassandra guitar, which was shipped back up north once the newspaper turned up evidence of a widow.

Yes, the widow. Was she grieving? No, except maybe for herself. Sara Gaunt was pregnant.

PART III

Men and Women

1

I play Delia a song. It's set in Memphis on the day Malcolm arrived, the day he met Eula. The day all that began. He was a sight for black shades, an ever-living marvel who could tie those guitar strings into fanciful bows, a man to make Sam Phillips a billion bucks and himself a nice pile, too. But he was pushing middle age, even if he didn't look it, and he was stepping into a Memphis where there lived this young thing who would be king.

The song is called "Elvis '53." It's about the King before he became something you couldn't take your eyes from. It's before his hillbilly superpowers were fully developed. It's before he had that last little bit of nerve it took to climb that stage and shake what Gladys gave him.

It's the song I was playing when I met Jimmy Lee. That was in

New York, the inevitable city. I'd left my small, gray city for the big, silver one. I'd set up on a sidewalk outside a bar called the Punk Cadillac. I played two Hank Williams weepers, an old Memphis blues, and that one of my own. I played loud and stomped feet. It was Cassie and me and a jangling of coins in a soft bed of dollar bills. When I finished, I looked up and there was Jimmy Lee Vine, standing there and shaking his head, saying if I wanted to make noise enough for two people what I needed was another person. He said he played electric guitar. I said, "Hell, you mean they make ones that plug in?" We introduced ourselves, shook hands, slapped backs—brothers in song, already. We walked inside the bar and drank eighteen dollars and change worth of beer, the box-office take of my little sidewalk show. We almost got drunk, on empty stomachs like we had.

Jimmy Lee had gotten to New York the same day, from Minnesota, but he had a friend in the city, so we went to see him. That was Buck. He had a little apartment with a furnished fridge, so we drank beer and played our music—it was our music, already. A guy who lived next door came to see what all the commotion was about. He said he thought it was a domestic disturbance of some sort and we thanked him for such high praise. Well, Jimmy Lee and I did. Buck just nodded to the fridge and the guy fell in with us. He became our bass player. His name was Mooney. He didn't stay on long enough for us to catch his full name. But he had a bass and he said he could play. So we became a band that night. We became the Long Gone Daddies. We didn't figure a rock 'n' roll band drunk on drink and history could go too far astray naming itself after a Hank Williams song. That, and there was something of a tradition in the Gaunt family line of daddies being long gone.

Delia shakes her head as I tell the tale. She takes the cigarette from her mouth and hangs a noose in the air. She says, "So did y'all play Madison Square Garden that first night, or was it the next week?"

We played street corners for change and small bills. We played subways, city parks, traffic jams, the sidewalk outside Yankee Stadium. I told the ball fans that Babe Ruth and Elvis Presley died on the same day, in different years. I said I didn't know what to make of that, but it's true. August 16. I said that day should be celebrated like a holiday, a holy day, mourned with kegs and candles. Even without me saying it was also the day of my own birth, hands reached into pockets and coins were dropped in an upturned Yankees cap. It was gas money, rambling fuel. We had a long haul ahead.

We fancied ourselves this brand-new thing, this unheard sound, this unsung song, all the while knowing we were the oldest story there was. We were Elvis all over again—that thick stew of country, blues, and gospel, whatever we could scrounge. Which made us what? A broken record? Fine.

So we decided to hit the road, to scavenge some more. To get what we could gather and make it our own. We drove in the general direction of Minnesota, Jimmy Lee's proud and native land. He lived in a small town called Busker. It's down the road from Hibbing, where you-know-who, Bob Dylan, grew up. So there we went. To Hibbing. We stopped, looked at Bob's house—the house we decided was his. I think the real one's gone, razed, but we couldn't have that. If the truth forsakes you, find some honest lie. That's what I say.

So we got out, stood and stared, soaked in the ambiance. There wasn't much. A little, was all. It was like Bob took it with him when he went. It was like he stuffed it in his pants pockets when he tramped out of town.

We breathed the air around Bob's old digs, didn't say much.

Jimmy Lee wanted to steal something, but the moment passed. Mooney just sat there moping. He'd been moping for several states. He was missing his girlfriend or the city or something. Next thing we knew, he up and walked away, never said a word. So we sat on the front stoop and drank a six-pack of Bunkhouse Beer. Cheap stuff, swill, not bad if it's good and cold; it wasn't. We sat and drank swill and talked music, the band. We wondered about wayward Mooney. We decided to stay a trio, at least for then. Because that's how Elvis started. Or maybe because we didn't have a fourth anymore. Mooney wasn't much of a bass player, truth be told. And anyway, it's easier to split a six-pack of beer among three. Bands have broken up over less.

"What happened to Mooney?" Delia says. "Still walking, you figure?"

"Well, we caught up with him on the way out of town. I guess he meant to walk all the way back to New York. We talked him back into the car and dropped him at the bus station. We gave him some money and he said we could keep that bass. He said to remember him when we got famous. We all had a good laugh over that."

Sweet Delia sighs. Sweet Delia stretches and cranes her neck. Sweet Delia has a pale, delicate, willowy, and winningly vulnerable neck. It's not the first thing you notice, but there it is.

"Famous," she says, as if that's the only word of the story she heard.

We fell in with the flow of the river, Old Man, the Mississippi, veering off for side trips. We followed all itches, urges, and wild hairs. Birthplaces, boyhood homes, crash sites. We drifted farther west than intended, gave fate free rein, ended up in Texas looking for Buddy Holly's ghost. We'd know him when we saw him.

"The one with black horn-rimmed glasses, you know," I say. "A sweet man, joy in his voice."

I take another glance at Texas Delia, there in the backseat. I go on with the story.

I tell how we played for drink money in an alley where Blind Lemon Jefferson did the same. So the story goes. That was in the town of Wortham. Then, in Dallas, Big D, we did our best T-Bone Walker on some Deep Ellum street corner. We played cities and small towns, your odd hamlet and whistle stop. We played tarpaper shacks, all-night diners, town-square gazebos. No venue too small for the Long Gone Daddies. We'd play the back of your hand, the small of your back. We spent one night in jail and played there, too. We hadn't done anything wrong—just broke, was all. We checked in like it was a motel. The jailer played stand-up bass and told stories of his own granddaddy traveling with Bob Wills and his Texas Playboys. I don't know if they were true stories, but they had that ring.

In San Antonio, we looked for the hotel where Robert Johnson recorded. Robert Johnson, who also died on that fated day, August 16. The hotel was gone, somebody said. But we stood for the longest time, sniffing mystery. And then off again. We drove through the night with the stereo blasting and the wind whipping like some ghostly horn section. We drove hours and didn't meet another set of headlights. Come dawn, we rolled into this dusty little town. Delia's town, dubbed Eden.

"So we stopped there to make a phone call," I say. "Jimmy Lee knows a guy who knows a guy who knows a guy in Memphis, and this last guy has a bar that might be looking for a band. I guess he never got around to making the call."

I turn to look at Delia. She's asleep. Buck's about out, too.

I nudge him enough that he lets his foot off the accelerator. The car eases off the road, about half into the ditch.

I wonder where we are, besides darkest Arkansas. I wonder if anything ever happened here, wonder was it some ancient bluesman's resting place one lost night.

The highway department could erect a plaque: *Robert Johnson slept it off here.*

A few hours later, pitch-black out, I feel a finger tap on my shoulder.

"Luther?"

"Yeah, Delia?"

She's half-asleep still, her voice low and scratchy like an old 78 rpm record.

"I want you to write me a song, okay?"

2

Jimmy Lee Vine looks like a matinee idol, along about dusk Sunday of a lost weekend. He's just that glamorous. He has long, coal-black hair he slings across his darkened face. He's a stick figure—the rock-star physique of choice—in tight black leather pants he bought in a secondhand store in Chicago.

Jimmy Lee sits up, rubs his eyes as Delia asks about our ambition. I'd been wondering how long that would take.

"Our ambition? You know, go to Memphis, make a record." Jesus, I sound like 1953.

Buck nods.

"And then." It's a command, not a question, the way she says it.

This one time, the drummer gets to sing lead. "Play it!" Buck says.

We laugh—all but Delia—but not because it's a joke. That's pretty much our version of fame, which has more than a sneaking resemblance to obscurity.

Delia frowns and taps a fresh cigarette on her bare knee. She says, "What about fame and money? You know, power, success, all that. What's so damn bad about double platinum? That's what you really want. You will, once you make a record. Get a little and you want a little more." She leans forward, ever more twang in her voice. The woman's tantalized by world domination.

"You've got to give people what they want, even if they don't know what it is yet," she says. "You've got to be easy on the eyes and easy on the ears. It's like, I don't know, the rules. The way things are. I haven't heard y'all play much, but . . . I don't know. Some polish to your sound—*our* sound. The right song, too. You need one to draw people in. You need one song the world can't get out of its head. And you, Luther, need to spiff it up, bud. Buck, you, too. Follow Jimmy Lee's lead. The boy knows you've got to look like a rock star if anybody's going to mistake you for one."

I'm wearing what I always wear: frayed blue jeans, T-shirt, old brown boots that look like they just stepped off of Penny's Farm. Buck's dressed likewise, except he's got on black high-top sneakers.

We take all this in. I guess it falls to the lead singer to give the band's official response.

"Well, sure, Delia, we want to be famous," I say. "But for doing what we're doing, for being who we are. We don't want to have to change our shirts, much less our songs. We want to be famous, I guess—but not for *being* famous or for being good looking. It's the music. It's the songs. They're sacred things, holy things. These songs are my religion. That's where I put my faith. I *believe* the songs. I don't believe much of what I'm told as gospel fact and I wouldn't trust the president of the United States as far as I could throw a preacher, but the songs . . . The *songs*, Delia."

"Really, now, Luther. I mean, fucking please," Delia says.

But I'm not quite through.

"This I believe, Delia: In songs I trust," I say. "Yeah, they've all been written, pretty much, but I'm not going to stop on that account. I'll just go on, in the family way. It's a responsibility and just about the only thing that's sacred to me. They've got to matter, mean something."

"Sacred," Delia says, as if it's the damnedest of all my many foolish notions.

"Okay, so I get a little carried away on the subject. But do you hear what I'm saying? Do you hear that I mean it? With us, it's the music. Am I making any sense here, Delia?" I stop and sigh. "What we're trying to do here is . . ."

And wonder, what the hell is it we're trying to do here, anyway?

Jimmy Lee lets the silence settle. He takes Delia's face in his hands and says, "Baby, we're going to put the bulge back in the pants of rock 'n' roll."

At which Buck slaps a bony knee and punches the accelerator and we go screaming down that Arkansas back road. I push a CD into the stereo—a something-fierce guitar jag, Howlin' Wolf himself, like to crawl out the speakers and devour us all.

We have a little moment, a sacred thing, but fuck's sake— now Delia's pouting. Who knew the woman had nuclear capability?

3

We make Hot Springs. We stop for the night in a roadside motel and spring for two rooms, Buck and me in one, Jimmy Lee and the world dominatrix in the other.

"Delia can screw your brains out, then we'll practice some," I say to Jimmy Lee. "See you in three minutes." I don't know why I'm turning on him. It's Delia, all Delia.

"Go to hell in a Dixie Cup, Luther."

I tell him I don't even know what that means. He looks at me like he'd like to punch me, but he's a guitar player and, you know, the hands.

We're not so good at fighting yet, see. Just feeling our way as we go.

4

The motel room smells of road sweat and cigarettes. It has this air—this stench—of folly and regret and something else I can't quite catch in the whiff I'm willing to take. The walls are papered beige, but the paper is peeling from them, fleeing them, really, from the top down and the bottom up. Buck opens the curtains to let in some light. That helps, but still it doesn't feel all that much like fame's waiting room.

I'm sitting on the end of the bed, playing the opening chords of my latest song. Jimmy Lee's sitting on the dresser, falling in step with me but speeding it up. I go slower. I make it a dirge, and Jimmy Lee a sprint.

"This thing got another gear, Luther?" Jimmy Lee says.

It's like one of us is climbing a hill and the other's tumbling down.

Buck stops beating his drumsticks on the overturned bucket he found in the bathroom and scrunches up his face.

Jimmy Lee stops, says, "Fuck it."

And I play the song myself:

> *Crucifix*
> *Guitar picks*
> *and Buddy Holly's glasses*

I stop and count three.

> *Pray God save our souls*
> *Pray God cover our asses*

"I hear a touch of high harmony in the last line there," I say. "Hint of gospel yearning, you know? Step on the word *cover*, soar just a little on *asses*. You think?"

Buck nods. Buck doesn't sing anyway.

"Yeah, well, whatever," Jimmy Lee says.

"Waste of time," Delia drawls. She's sitting in an old, over-stuffed easy chair in the corner of the room, arms draped over the bass. It looks like she's auditioning us, seeing if we're worthy of playing her coronation.

"Huh?"

"That won't get played on the radio. Not with *God* and *asses* in the same damn line."

"Delia's right," Jimmy Lee says.

I shoot him a glare. I stare daggers and buckshot and kitchen knives.

So Jimmy Lee says to Delia, "Well, it's not God's ass he's talking about."

I smile. That's my boy. Trying to have it both ways, in the grand tradition of man.

Delia stands, whirls and turns and bangs out of the room.

The bass falls, plays a sort of note as it hits the floor. Jimmy Lee starts to follow, but she's already slammed the door. He sits back down, shakes his head. Buck gives the bucket a whack and stops. The Long Gone Daddies do have the damnedest time keeping a bass player.

A few seconds pass and the phone sounds. Jimmy Lee smothers it in one ring. He mostly just listens and then hangs up and says, "Delia said she's willing to give it another try when you're willing to change your attitude and open your mind to someone else's artistic vision. That's what she said. Those words."

"She's mad at *me*? You're the one who said the thing about God's ass."

"You wrote the song, brother."

5

I awake to silence, not an altogether unpleasant sound. Silence is great, silence is good, we thank silence for this mood. I stumble across the room in the dark, crawl into jeans and my boots, throw on an old shirt. I stretch and yawn. I await an urge or an itch or perhaps some holy apparition. We never did see Buddy Holly's ghost, after all.

I peek out the curtain—coast clear. Clear of what, I don't know. Talent scouts. Groupies. Autograph seekers. I walk outside and across the parking lot and into a diner.

Cup of coffee, black as a vinyl record.

Biscuits and gravy.

And yours very truly, perched wearily on a wobbly stool at the counter. There's nothing on the jukebox but mainstream country, lots of spiff and polish. I play one at random. The cook, thin and haggard, sings along. His voice is all cigarettes and double shots. But raw is real, my daddy used to say. The cook sings the truth and saves the song. So there's a song underneath all that polish. I wonder, does the polish come in fifty-five-gallon drums? I wonder, does Nashville just dip in the records, or dunk the singers whole?

The waitress, a small drink of something stout and sour, says he's ruining the song, says he's going to run away all the customers. Which at the moment is me, and I'm not going anywhere.

"I kind of like his singing," I say.

She glares.

I shrug and say, "Customer's always right, right?"

The cook goes for a high note and doubles over in a fit of coughs and laughter. He sounds like TB, over easy, side of black lung. I love this guy tremendously. I want to marry his daughter, have his grandchildren, raise them on greens and slapback.

The cook finally stands, listing first one way, then another. There's a nametag on his shirt. His name is Roland.

"I was some kind of hot-shit rockabilly sumbitch in my day," Roland says. "Memphis called out to me."

"And I'm Natalie Wood," the waitress says, shaking her head. "Faked my death and here I am, lying low."

"Hell of a disguise, woman." He grins at me, his teeth gray and dingy in crooked, tombstone rows.

She tops off my coffee and I say thanks. I roll my eyes with hers. We're in cahoots now. She has a pot of scalding coffee in her gun hand; I side with whoever holds the weapon.

"In my day . . . ," the cook says again. "In my day . . ."

She leans in to me and says, "Sumbitch never had a day. He had a night, and it was Saturday. All he got out of it was a hangover."

I can see her nametag now. It doesn't say Natalie. It says Vivian. She's still leaning in. She's wearing perfume, but the scent of bacon grease is on her already, or on her still.

She says into my right ear, "Tell me something I don't know, hon."

"Johnny Cash sold vacuum cleaners and other appliances door to door," I say, because Vivian was the name of Johnny's first wife. "That's what he was doing when, you know, he became Johnny Cash."

"Tell me more," she says, and so I tell the tale of Johnny and Vivian.

"They met at a roller rink in Texas, I think it was," I say. "It was a true story of young love that took but didn't hold. She was a dark beauty, some thought black, and they were a good-looking couple. They were big-screen, hot-shit good looking. Johnny wrote 'I Walk the Line' for Vivian. But he wanted to play that music, too—*had* to play that music—and so he was out there on the road all the time. There was bad stuff out on that road. There were pills enough to raise the Southern war dead. Johnny took them all. He came near to killing himself, living like that. But then June, you know. June Carter, the love of his life. Sweet June. She saved him. Vivian gave Johnny a divorce and June married him. It wasn't tidy like that sounds, but it happened."

She's still leaning in to me. Cahoots, it turns out, is not the most desirable place to be with Miss Vivian. But she's still got the pot of coffee in her hand. *Play it smart now, Luther boy. Stay calm. No false moves and nobody gets his pecker scalded off.*

Now the bells on the door jangle: Delia in her glory, a long, tall tale of Texas limbs and wiles, all curves and swells and ample skin of pale. Delia, Delia, Delia. She's a threat to world peace before breakfast, even.

"You told me yours, now I'll tell you mine," she says. "Life story, I mean. Then you'll write me a song. So there'll be no doubt but what it's mine."

Delia glances up and down the menu, tells Viv she'll take eggs over real light, sausage links, bacon with a bit of wiggle, biscuits slathered with gravy, short stack of cakes, milk, orange juice, deep well of strong, black coffee.

"So just some of everything, then," Vivian says with a sneer that sends fissures through her pancake makeup.

Delia shows Vivian a pained smile from her vast collection.

"And why would I do that?" I say to Delia.

"Because that's what songwriters do. They write songs for singers to sing. The songs go up the charts, everybody makes piles of money, and we all live happily ever after on big estates outside Nashville."

"I write songs for the band," I say. "Then I sing them. It's a band. Maybe you forgot. I should paint it on the side of the Merc—*Long Gone Daddies*. So there'd be no doubt, as you say."

"I play bass, Luther."

"Well, you stand there and hold the thing like it's your latest flame. You look good doing it. You don't actually play the thing much, which doesn't put you all that far behind our pal Mooney, technically speaking."

"It's not my life's ambition to be the bass player in this band, Luther."

"Well, it's my life's ambition to front it. I'll be happy to play out my days this way. It's my thing. It's my little gig in this screwed ol' world."

"Ain't the world that's screwed, Luther. Listen to you. You're scared. That's all the hell it is. You're scared of fame and money and having that spotlight come anywhere near you. Like the spotlight's some death ray or something. You're scared like your daddy was. I don't know if your daddy's daddy was, too. But it had to start somewhere. I'm sorry, Luther. But look at yourself. You may be the biggest coward of the whole damn lot. You hide in this little band. You hide in this little band with cool songs but no gumption, and you put dirty sacrilege in them—in the damn chorus—just to make double sure the radio won't play them. Not that I've got anything against dirty. But Jesus, Luther. I mean, *Jesus*."

I don't say anything to all that. I just let the minutes pass until Delia's breakfast arrives in a row of plates and saucers running up Vivian's right arm. Delia stabs her eggs, watches them run. I go and play a few songs on the jukebox, to give her the slicked-up soundtrack her life story surely will require.

"My daddy was a man of the cloth," Delia says. "Satin sheets, more often than not."

I laugh and we fall into something like a temporary truce. I turn full around to hear her tale of woe and smut, leaning on the counter. I'm on pins and elbows. I'm a sucker for my-daddy's-a-fuckup-how-about-yours stories. This is a pretty fair one, as they go. Daddy the evangelist has a thing for the ladies of the choir. Ladies of the choir have a thing for Daddy back, but on the sly, unbeknownst to each other. Nothing stays unbeknownst for long, so jealous husbands with shotguns begin to hover. All run and duck for cover. It's like a square dance with firearms. I sense a song in it. The good reverend daddy decides to take his ministry on the road, all the better to stay one step ahead. Alabama to Louisiana and on into Texas. Beaumont. Abilene. Ass Scratch. Wherever souls cry out for salvation. He leaves Delia and her mama, the latter a tall, solemn woman who pines for Jesus.

"She was always going on about our Savior," Delia says. "She said He was coming one day. And then she'd look out the window, like our Savior just pulled up in a wood-panel station wagon and here she was, with her hair a mess and her one good dress in the wash."

So Delia, with a fraud and a fanatic for parents, started to rebel. She says, "I guess any normal, healthy teenager of the species would have."

Well, good people: It's one of the particular joys of this earth to hear a girl in full Southern twang say that word *species*. You can have your hymns and arias and your Symphony no. 3 in E flat, op. 55.

Delia says her mama had visions of Jesus Christ—she'd see him everywhere, in the living-room carpet, on toast. Delia would come for a look and declare them to be dead ringers for local winos, famous gunslingers of yore, the odd Rolling Stone.

She listened to rock 'n' roll. But for kicks, she played old records she found in a closet. She could sing along to those, slow and mournful as they were: country torch and other slow burns. She found her voice to be not altogether unpleasant. It was the first thing about herself she liked—she says she was a skinny little thing in those days, plain, a wallflower. But then that voice, the sound of the thing. She holed up in her room, sat on the window sill, sang out the window. She learned to lose some of that twang she got from growing up all over; she learned to control it, use it when she wanted. Plain-looking girls sitting on window sills in Eden, Texas, don't get discovered. But still she sang. She sang Patsy and Loretta. She sang train songs, cowboy ballads. She sang gospel.

Delia sighs—a little overly dramatic, I suspect, but maybe that's just me, starting to get suspicious. She drops her head.

Fade out.

And now a word from our sponsors.

But Delia raises her head and turns toward me, her face half-hidden by her long, thick vines of dirty-blond hair. She wants me to part the vines, come inside, and see what danger lurks there. She wants me to want to, is mostly what it is, I think.

I snap out of it, tell myself I do.

"Then one day," she says, "I woke up with this body and this face. It was almost like it happened overnight. That was summer, and when summer ended and school started up again, everything was different. I tormented the local boys something lethal just by walking down the halls. Not that I stopped at that. I let them think I was the party girl, every red-blooded boy's dream of a preacher's long-legged daughter, all the while keeping most of my clothes on. Mostly. I was biding my time. I knew, Luther Gaunt. I knew for the first time."

"Knew what, Delia?"

"Knew my time would come."

Delia crosses those long legs of hers. I notice, not because I'm staring or anything, the rose tattoo on her pale right thigh. It's quite a rose, quite a thigh; the thorns are a nice touch, for those who like their metaphors sharp and prickly.

"Anyway," she says, "that's a pretty fair version of the truth. I'm not the fraud my daddy is, but I inherited his, let's say, initiative. I'm my mama's little lost girl, too, so I'm a bit of a fanatic."

She stops, lets a serious calm come between us. She gets close and says in a low, chilling tone, "So listen to me, Luther goddamn Gaunt: I want fame and wealth and spotlights and magazine covers and my own Nashville billboard and I most especially want a guitar-shaped swimming pool—see, boy, I'm just an old-fashioned girl—and I will by hell have it all, every bit."

She raises her last piece of bacon. It has a bit of wiggle in it, just like she ordered.

The diner is filling up now, weary travelers sprung from the floor tiles. Roland, the one-time, hot-shit rockabilly sumbitch, has his thin, hunched back to us, his right elbow flying, eggs crackling like a short-wave broadcast.

We pay Vivian, who's gone businesslike on us and is busy besides, so she doesn't call me hon and doesn't tell me to tell her something she doesn't know. I was going to tell her Minnie Pearl came from a rich family and went to finishing school. I tell Delia instead, as we walk across the parking lot.

"I guess the finish came off," she says, leaving me behind.

Delia takes long strides with those endless legs and I hurry to keep up. My feet fall with thuds, heels scuffing, toes scraping. Some people are hell on wheels. I'm hell on shoes.

At her motel-room door, I say, "I think there's a song in all that, Delia. Or a morality play, one. Anyway, it's nice to know where you come from and where you're going. It's nice to know we're just a cab you hailed to take you there." I try for a tone of disgust, but there's a thread of defeat I hope Delia doesn't notice. I'd rather keep the thread to myself. Get enough and I'll have a spiffy new shirt, or a surrender flag.

Delia puts her right hand to my face, her thumb below my chin and fingers fanned out across my cheek. She kisses me—it's the damnedest kiss, a peck that lingers. I take it like a man.

"It's not like that, Luther," she says after. "I want Jimmy Lee and I need you. But for different reasons. Buck just plain makes me nervous. I'd feel better if you took custody of the ice pick."

She opens the motel-room door and I see Jimmy Lee, naked, sprawled across the bed, watching TV through tired slits of lazy eyes. I hear cartoon voices, popcorn gunfire.

She says, "I'll leave you to write my song and you'll leave me to my man. So run along now, do what you do."

I walk next door. Buck's disappeared. He's prone to that.

The TV's on with the sound down and a preacher, red-faced and square-jawed, is about to come busting through the screen. A phone number and P.O. box move across the screen: Send your donations now, all you lost souls and heathen sinners.

I sit on the edge of the bed, before the preacher and God and the air-conditioner hum. I strum.

6

I start lightly on the strings, wondering where Cassie falls on the subject of Delia and her fame craving. I wonder if they're rivals or if they're in cahoots. I wonder if Delia is the human embodiment of the guitar, the living, breathing, humping, bitching, moaning, slinking, ass-shaking, tits-in-a-T-shirt *she*.

Impossible. It must be so.

I graze the strings. *Now, now.* This is with my right hand. My left circles around the back of the neck, sneaking up on the thing, trying to take it by calm. *Here, here.* There are gods and goddesses of possibilities, my daddy used to say, and they are giving, but sometimes grudgingly so. They are not to be fooled with or otherwise sassed. *Yeah, baby. Yeah.*

Chords begin to suggest themselves. Sound becomes song.

Cassie, an old-fashioned girl herself, seems to have just the number for our Delia.

And so the words. The first is the hardest. The second is mere death struggle.

Well . . .

The TV preacher has slumped on the stage, down to his knees. His eyes are clenched, face red and sweating. He lets the microphone drop and roll away. The crowd rises, rushes the stage, thinking . . . what? Heart attack? Judgment Day? Latest script twist? And I think about love, fear, hate, and commerce, about endless legs, and pecks that linger. I think about possibilities and goddesses bearing gifts and grudges; I wonder if I could tell the one from the other.

The song starts as a slow shuffle and then stops, seems to ponder itself as a full-tilt rave-up, reluctantly resumes its shuffle. You never do know about songs. You follow them where they go, to the edges of cliffs, down blind alleys, off the sides of bridges, to the brink, the bank, the barroom, and then . . .

I open my mouth to see what comes out—shards of garble, bits of fragments, odds of ends. An hour passes like a procession, and then one word takes up where another leaves off.

Well . . .

Carl Perkins, my daddy's favorite, said every rockabilly song begins with that word. Some other sorts of songs do, too. My daddy loved the way Carl played guitar. In his hands, it was a train clattering on down the tracks. Carl could take you places. Carl could get you there fast. It was leaving music.

> *Well, she left under cover*
> *of dusk and indifference*
> *an East Texas town*
> *of rust, dust, and dirt*
>
> *They said she could sing*
> *like an angel forsaken*
> *a voice to make you*
> *forget where it hurt*

*Singing, "I don't ache for your touch
I just don't care that much
I don't quake
I don't quiver
I don't swoon
I don't melt
when you walk in the room"*

Mostly, my daddy loved that Carl just sang his songs and lived a life. He didn't become Elvis. The world didn't hold deed on his soul. No man who called himself "Colonel" had him on a string or leash. Carl could lie low in plain sight.

I guess my daddy knew the truth behind all that—that Carl tried to be as big as Elvis, but that fate and other things interceded. There was that car wreck Carl and his brothers had on the way to New York City for that TV appearance. "Blue Suede Shoes" was on the charts and Carl was on his way, a man playing guitar like a train clattering on down the tracks. But while he was in the hospital for repairs, the world changed, seemed to leave him behind. My daddy would say Carl was better off getting his life back and paying no more cost than a few broken bones.

*She sang over clangs
of beer mugs and ashtrays
two sets a night
at the Rose Tattoo*

*Well, record moguls
they're dim but they're thirsty
one saw her and said,
"I'll make a star out of you"*

Singing, "I don't ache for your touch

I just don't care that much
I don't quake
I don't quiver
I don't swoon
I don't melt
when you walk in the room"

And there's Delia, who's got fame on order, who will have it. There's Delia, who wants a song: this song, old-fashioned but dipped in gloss, given a sheen and sent on down the assembly line with not a train's clatter but a smooth, cold, automated hum.

Well, the world fell down
down at her feet now
lifted her up
paved gold to the coast

There was fame, there were movies
but always the songs
and the one she sang best
was the one she meant most

Singing, "I don't ache for your touch
I just don't care that much
I don't quake
I don't quiver
I don't swoon
I don't melt
when you walk in the room"

Delia, Delia, Delia. You sweet, evil Delia.

I sing through the verses again, scribble on motel stationery as I go. Before the thing ever reaches anyone's airwaves, I suspect, a sharp knife will be taken to the line about the dim mogul. He'll have a brilliant ear for the human voice and soul. And as for liquor, he won't touch the stuff.

> *Alone at the top*
> *the one and lonely*
> *an angel forsaken*
> *by chance and*
> *by choice*

Then these words, spoken:

> *Well, the fates, they do love*
> *to serve us*
> *just right*
> *The fates, they do seem*
> *to have a way*
> *with things*
> *But the one thing the fates*
> *love above all else*
> *is to hear a sad singer*
> *is to hear a sad song*

And once more with the chorus, once more with the hook.

Now the TV preacher stirs. He rises and reaches one hand toward the ceiling. The camera pans to the choir and I can hear the voices even with the sound down. I strum along. The screen goes to snow and I stop in its tracks, lost. But that being no good reason to stop, I trudge on. I sing that chorus again.

I'm watching the TV screen as I play. It's snowy still. The screen is the color of doubt, but now the snow clears and I see where the song has gone—to the cliff, of course. A cliffhanger it is.

I set aside the old family guitar. I scribble all the rest I can remember. I crumple the paper and toss it in the guitar case. I wonder how Delia would sound singing it, wonder would it, could it, be a Nashville smash. I wonder how it would sound after it's been dipped in industrial-strength sheen and commercial-grade gloss, the words lost in service to the tune, the story to the message, the message being only this: Buy me.

I don't know and don't care. But . . .

It's a cautionary tale. It's a lament and a prophecy and the best I can do, under circumstances unforeseen. Working title: "I Don't Melt."

Says me to myself: *Tell me something I don't know.*

7

Back on the road. The cattle are lowing. Some are. A few gather by the fence to watch, death-eyed, as the car blows by.

Weatherman on the radio says it's coming a storm. I close my eyes, batten those hatches.

I dream I'm standing in a field. I'm alone. It's summer, and dusk, mosquitoes cleared for landing. I kick at a clump of dirt, as if there's a clue inside, or a diamond. But the dirt becomes dust and settles on the tips of my shoes. I'm wearing old brown things, what they used to call brogans. Now I hear the notes and see the neon, far across the field. Flat as the land is, it might be days away, ages. The notes are slow, droning, and blue. A heavy foot stomps time, a woman screams, and in the scream is sheer delight—sexual abandon and the house's best hooch.

It's a clapboard shack and seems almost to sway as I move toward it. But for each step I take, I lose two. The neon grows dim and the music faint and I stop and look for another clump of dirt to kick. But it's dark now. I sit, close my eyes, and await the next scene, or a new dream.

I awake to gray skies, crossroads.

"Go south, young Buck," I say, and I go back to sleep, back to dreaming, pleasantly this time: Patsy Cline's smoking a cigarette and singing "Crazy" about me, the dress she wore at Carnegie Hall, New York City, November 29, 1961, a-pile on the carpet.

"Lay down that damn guitar, boy," she says. "You'll be needing both hands for ol' Patsy."

The sky swirls. The sky tries for ever-darker shades, some lost middle ground between gray and black. Delia, awake and restless, says, "Play some sex music."

"It's all sex music," I say. "The bottleneck blues and the slow, country shuffle and the stark-raving rockabilly. Any song or sound." I turn up the radio: the farm report, hog futures.

"Hey, I'm turned on," Jimmy Lee says.

"*Men.*" Delia spits out the word as if it were milk that's soured.

"Fuck's that supposed to mean?" Jimmy Lee says.

Delia is wearing an old cowboy shirt with some lariat-looking design on it, and it's too big for her, and one shoulder is showing where it sort of falls off her—and when exactly, good people, did I become a shoulder man? And Delia, she's barefoot with her hair stuffed wild up under a black ball cap with the proud emblem of some farm-implement concern emblazoned across the front. She's draped across Jimmy Lee.

"*Men,*" she says again, a bit mean this time.

I let it pass like a long, black train full of steam and menace, but Jimmy Lee persists.

"You mean all men," he says, "or just Luther and the like?"

"Men," she says again, but more as a sigh. "Simple, bumbling things. Wear your tails on the front and think, *Ain't that just something?* Think we ought to get down on our damn knees and give thanks."

Never one to lie down on train tracks unduly, I let that one pass, too. I'm not sure, at any rate, what exception I'd take. I make no great claims for the male of the species. I consider myself simple and bumbling on a good day. As for the bit about the tails, well, I'd only venture the girl's been paying attention. I think, *We're helpless, hopeless, hapless, but somebody has to do it. We're bullies and we're imbeciles and we're bastard fucks. Men.*

A homemade CD is playing, one of our own, a scruffy, ambling road song:

> *I'm an old car battered*
> *I'm frayed-flag tattered*
> *Been awhile since I mattered*
> *to you*

Jimmy Lee, meanwhile, presses ever onward, inching up onto the tracks, into the dank shadow of male folly.

"I respect women," he says. "I'm in awe of women. It's not about flesh and curves and angles with me. It's about the little things, you know. Your lip curled, Delia, and about to say something sweet. Hand on your hip when you're pissed. Your eyes when they're just peeking out on a new day. Mostly, well, it's about what's inside. The curves are about the seventeenth thing I even notice. The angles are along about, oh, twenty-third. So don't talk to me about *men*. I'm not *men*—I'm a man and I'm different. I'm Jimmy Lee Vine."

For a simple man without much to say generally, it's a damn eloquent discourse. Even the most generous of listeners, though, could count half a dozen lies in it. Hell, Jimmy Lee's last name isn't even really Vine.

"Oh, yeah, that's you, Jimmy Lee," I say. "Always looking for the inner bombshell."

Delia yanks him atop her. "You'll do," she says, "for now."

8

Up the road, we stop so I can use a pay phone.

"Hello?"

"Hey, Ma."

"Luther, where are you?"

"Oh, you know, here and there. The Southern states."

We're at an old roadside grocery. The pay phone's out front. There's not much traffic, just the occasional pickup truck hauling nothing, going nowhere. This part of Arkansas could use some rain to tamp down the dust.

"Headed for Memphis, you mean."

I try to make out the weary smile on the other end of the line. "Ah, Ma."

"You always were a good boy, Luther. You're a good man. You know? There's nothing wrong with that. There's not a thing in the world wrong with that."

"You getting at something, Ma?"

"No. Yes. Just . . . I don't know, Luther. I just don't want you to think you have to be what they were. Maybe they couldn't help themselves, once they got that damn guitar in their hands. They'd follow it—"

"Her. That's how it was to them, I mean. I know better. I'm just saying."

"Right, right. Her. They'd follow her anywhere. They'd . . ."

Delia comes up behind, takes me by the belt buckle, and pulls me close. I turn without realizing, without thinking, to kiss her, but instead I get a swig of beer from a quart bottle in a brown paper bag. I've had worse kisses.

Now she knocks me one—nothing in the kiss, though, but tease and devilment, trace elements of cheap beer and Arkansas grocery-store dope. It's then I notice the joint in her other hand, still down about my belt buckle. She lifts it to my lips and whispers into my ear, "Tell Mama your girlfriends Cassie and Delia say, 'Hey, Mama.' "

"Luther?"

"Tell her they've got her boy good and whipped."

"Luther?"

I cough and sputter. "Yeah. Yeah, Ma. I'm here. I'm just . . ."

Just what, Luther Gaunt? Drinking beer and smoking weed in Broad Daylight, Arkansas, while your band mate's best girl whispers devilment and dope-speak in your ear?

"I've got a touch of something."

As lies go, it's within driving distance of true. It will have to do, anyway.

My ma lets it go. She says, "Well, anyway."

"Yeah, I know, Ma. I know what you're saying. I do. I'll take care of myself. I'll be, you know, good. I try, is the main thing. I think so. I don't know. I love you, Ma."

I hang up.

I say, "The devil would run at the very sight of you, Delia Shook." I'd run, too, if she'd just let loose of my belt buckle.

"The devil bores me. He's only ever got one thing on his mind. I prefer you. You're a complicated boy."

"You mean you prefer Jimmy Lee. Where is he, anyway?"

Jimmy Lee Vine—real name, Mince—is inside, probably reading the new *Rolling Stone*. He likes to imagine he'll come across some mention of the Long Gone Daddies. Buck apparently is in there negotiating down the price of Delia's dope from the teenage counter help.

"You're a challenge—mostly to yourself. Kind of fun to watch you struggle, though. Almost sweet, if I was into that kind of stuff. You've got some things in you I haven't much seen before. Integrity. Honesty. You'll be better off once they're out of your system, but the fact they're in there makes you interesting to me. Like I say, a complicated boy."

She lets loose of the belt buckle. I stand up straight, look her in the eye. She lifts the joint again to my lips.

"You want another hit on this?" she says.

Buck guides the Merc down Highway 49, east into Mississippi and the fabled Highway 61, the crossroads there, where we'll head south—the wrong way, if you're Memphis-bound—for a little side trip.

9

Clarksdale now. It's a sly little town. There, amid the convenience stores, repair shops, and ice-cream stands, you see the odd juke joint—the Lean Mean House of Soul, the Rooster Lounge, Uncle Slake's—and there's a blues museum where impressionable youth can stare at a life-size model of Muddy Waters on a little stage and peruse the dirty lyrics from cutting contests.

We spend the afternoon in the museum. I do, Buck does. Delia leaves after an hour with Jimmy Lee in tow. I flip through old magazines, studying pictures as if looking for leads. Take away the state of Mississippi and twentieth-century America couldn't carry a tune. Muddy. Jimmie Rodgers—the Singing Brakeman, America's Blue Yodeler, the Father of Country Music. Elvis the King. Howlin' Wolf, Robert Johnson, and Son House. Charley Patton's gravelly chant. Skip James with that high whine straight out of hell's choir. Furry Lewis. The Mississippi Sheiks. Bo Diddley and his wild-hair beat.

I find a chair in the corner. I close my eyes and conjure a cutting contest between Muddy and Elvis, the lord-god of all cutting contests, could be staged only at the crossroads or the gates of hell. No, Madison Square Garden.

I stare across the room and see through slits of eyes the model of Muddy, dressed in gray pinstripe suit and baby-blue tie, come to life. His head bobs, his foot thumps high time, and he sings,

> *Well, Elvis' woman drop him*
> *She drop him like a ton uh bricks*
> *But Elvis still see her every day*
> *out front of Graceland turnin' tricks*

Elvis, all curled lip and black leather, sings back,

> *Well, Muddy, your baby come to see me*
> *She seemed to know the way*
> *She said, "Elvis, drop the needle*
> *Oh, sweet Elvis, let the record play"*

Muddy pulls back and surveys all that's before him—his first acknowledgment that he's not strumming away a lazy summer Sunday afternoon on the front porch of his Coahoma County sharecropper's cabin.

He sings,

Well, Elvis, your baby's nice and tall
and her skin all pale and soft
I say, "Why Elvis buy you that nice dress, babe,
if you just gonna take it off?"

Elvis slaps his knee as the sold-out crowd thunders. Elvis quiets it with a raised hand and sings,

Well, we did it in Muddy's cabin
We did it in Muddy's bed
Muddy's gal lay there satisfied
"First time for everythin," she said

Muddy arches his head, stares past Elvis and the crowd, conjures words from the far corners of the rafters:

Well, we did it in the alley
and we did it at the fair
Well, we did it down on Beale Street
and Lord, we did it in midair

Then we did it in the Jungle Room
while Elvis he was asleep
and we did it in the Graceland basement
Elvis' girl say, "Muddy, you so deep"

Elvis drops his head and grins. His hands fly from the guitar and he becomes an airplane that's lost a wing and is going down. Then he pulls up, two feet from the ground, turns a little flip, rights himself, and sings,

Well, Muddy's woman had an hour
He give her a minute of his time

She came to me, said, "Elvis,
won't you fill the other fifty-nine?"

I filled her every minute
I give her seconds, too,
and when my clock struck straight-up noon
I swear, Mud, time's not all that flew

Elvis looks up, cocks his head, curls his lip again. He lets his lids fall heavy upon tired eyes. Someone, quick, commission a sculpture.

Muddy sees the curled lip and raises an eyebrow. He sings,

She say, "I took all Elvis give me
I wanted ten, he give me five
I come crawlin' now to you, Big Muddy,
I need me a man alive"

And so I give her what she wanted
I give her candle, flame, and wick
She say, "All Elvis ever give me
is the short end of the stick"

The house rocks, city shakes. Elvis falls to the floor in mock pain. He pulls from his black folds of leather a white handkerchief, waves it. Muddy stands over him, helps him up. Both stand and bow, all applaud. They walk off, split the take.

And someone shakes me awake.

My eyes open to Buck. His nod says the place is closing, time to go. Time to see a cabin about a man.

We walk outside. Delia's stretched across the hood of the Merc, sunning herself, boots propped on the steer horns. Buck, perturbed, goes to straighten them. If they're positioned just so, you can tell the time and the future.

Jimmy Lee meets me at the stoop of the building. "Delia says—"

"Delia's all the time saying things," I say. "She's going to be the death of this band, you know. She's using you and she's using me. She wants me to write her a song. I haven't even heard her sing. Have you?"

"Well, she sort of coos in my ear sometimes." Jimmy Lee is not above being used, if there's something in it for him. "But yeah, I know."

"And when she gets what she wants, she's gone. After she's gone, I don't know if anything will be the same. With us, all of us. The band."

"Well, I say we just ride it out," Jimmy Lee says.

"Ride, huh?"

"It's more than that, Luth. Look at her. If she can sing half as good as she can coo, she's going places that Merc won't take the likes of us."

"And if she's just using us to get there?"

"Well, I vote again to ride it out."

"You get to vote only once. What's Buck say?"

"Buck doesn't. Shrugs and nods, is all. He'll go as we go. So what about you?"

I force a smile. "Be a shame to quit before we get to Memphis. But I'm telling you, I see bad things happening. I see us in shambles and Delia off getting what Delia wants next."

"Brother, we need to seriously see about getting you laid."

I don't doubt Delia's power to destroy us, but I do wonder what makes her—what makes *me*—think I can come up with a Nashville-slick hit song. Can I go that low and strike that chord? Can I do it just once and stop?

I sit and watch Delia as she stretches out, hands through her hair, the sun having its way with her curves. I watch her watching me watching her.

I seriously need to see about getting laid.

10

You luck upon the right road out of town. You follow the curve of its bends into the countryside. That's how you find Muddy Waters's cabin. There it is, on the left, at the top of a small rise, twenty feet off the road.

"Is this it?" Delia wants to know.

"You expecting gates like Graceland? You expecting a mansion? This is where it all began. This is where the song starts, right here. Listen."

It's a tiny cabin. There's not room enough to change your mind.

"Look at this place," I say. "Jesus."

"Away in a manger," Delia drawls, "no crib for Mud's bed."

There's nothing to it, really. Just a few planks of wood held together by an aura. Touch it and it comes off in your hands, little splinters of ancient wood and history.

It's hazy. Late afternoon. I sit cross-legged on the grass, pull out a cigarette. I light it with all the calculated crawl of ritual. I half-expect the smoke to smell like incense.

"This is church," I say. "My church."

I say this to Delia, who's come by to bum a cigarette.

"This is religious ground. County seat of the Holy Land. One of them. There are a few. Muddy's cabin. Sun Records. Graceland. The abandoned movie theater that became the home of Stax Records. Holy Lands. You feel it, Delia?"

"Damn hot and hazy," Delia says, wiping sweat with the sleeve of her cowboy shirt. "I feel that."

"Close enough," I say, smiling.

Buck stands in the doorway, looking through to the other side, where Jimmy Lee's peering in. You can't go inside. It's blocked off. There's a sign warning of bad mojo for anyone who fucks with the old homestead.

"So Muddy shook the ground, did he?"

"He shook the ground and loosened the roots. The greatest, some say."

"And you, Luther Gaunt, little white altar boy of the First Church of Mud. What do you say?"

"Well, it depends on the day, my mood. Generally, it's a dead heat between Muddy and Robert Johnson. Those two, and then the others. But they're different, you know. Robert scares me. His voice does. I buy into all that devil business, because it's there in the songs. The man was haunted. Possessed. No one sounds like that. It's the sound of the soul as damaged goods. But Muddy, he was a sort of royalty. He was the boss, the king."

I light another cigarette. I light one for Delia. She moves in close to take it. Her hair brushes my cheek and in the moment I forget her agenda, her lust for fame, her hidden switches and trapdoors. She smiles and it's a real smile. I tell myself so. I tell myself, *She's a good listener. Nobody listens anymore.*

"Robert may have sold his soul," I say, "but Muddy, he cut a better deal. Robert was desperate, would've agreed to anything. He needed the power that was inside the guitar. Guitars, hollow as they are, can hide all sorts of secrets. Muddy was born with the goods. He just needed the break, the opportunity, a light to move toward. He just needed to be discovered and needed to get the hell out of the Delta, if it meant driving a tractor all the way to Chicago." I turn to face her, wag my cigarette at her. "I see Muddy at the crossroads, standing straight and tall, saying to the devil, 'No, motherfucker, *you* listen to *me*.' Listen to the records and you can hear it. Robert is possessed. Muddy *possesses*."

Delia taps her cigarette against mine, says, "To dead heats, Luther Gaunt."

I stand and give her a hand up. She looks me in the eye, doesn't say anything.

Buck and Jimmy Lee join us and we all stare. We all have a little moment. Delia pulls out a joint and we fire it up and pass it about.

We drift away, one by one, to the car. I'm last.

"I'm coming. Be there in a minute."

I'm waiting for a voice. I'm waiting for the echoes of orders, a sign or vision. I'm waiting for the ghost of Muddy, or God, or the devil, or some closer kin, to give me . . . what? The stamp of approval. Battle plans. Marching orders. Yes, all that.

But nothing.

I walk to the car and climb in.

"Let's cut it," I say, and Buck cranks the engine.

11

Muddy made whiskey. Muddy drove a tractor. Muddy had house parties in his cabin, played his blues, and made a little scratch. He took a woman not his wife to St. Louis, to the big city, but it didn't feel right and he came back. Came back home and told his wife to move out. Sometime later, he left again, this time for Chicago. The rest you know.

We're in and out of Clarksdale proper. Dark now. On the edge of town, Buck wheels into a little juke called Mamie's Last Word, a once-white, shingled shack with an oak tree growing out of the center. A blues band is howling in the far corner, the front man crawling inside a harmonica as if demons are in there and they've stolen his wallet. There is an absolute madcap glee in the tone.

Mamie greets us at the front door with a smile and a metal detector.

The bar has a dirt floor.

We're dancing, Delia and I, bare feet on brown earth. She's dancing. I'm swaying and lurching, feet barely moving. Delia says I dance like a man in shackles who's climbed out on a ledge and doesn't know what to do next.

Why did the man in shackles climb out on the ledge? Because he heard a song out there.

Delia turns to liquid as she dances. What a tall drink of the strong stuff she is. She moves as if poured from a jug of Muddy's homemade hooch. The bar is packed, everyone dancing, and she pulls me into the middle and commences a dance I'll call, for lack of a given Christian name, Simulated Sex Act.

She's up against me, up and down me. I'm hard-pressed to resist. Well, I'm hard and I'm pressed. She begins that cooing thing she does.

I wonder where Jimmy Lee is, but before I see him I hear him—hear his guitar, the ragged tangle of notes. He's sitting in with the band. He's sitting in with the band while his girlfriend does a full-body search for the hit country tune I'm thought to have on my person.

"You want to take this outside?" I hear one of us say.

Out back in a field. We fall in with the beat of the song, the thump of the thing. Delia brings me to my buckling knees as the band slows the song to a simmer. Delia gives me no small shove. She's strong, not a fragile, skinny, breakable thing. She's strong like a river. She's current and undertow. She's murk and flow and depth. She'll take you under, boys.

She's atop me, and I realize she's changed back into Jimmy

Lee's pink satin shirt. Not sure when that happened, but I know why. And so one button, two, and three. She sheds the shirt, hangs it from the half-moon.

I say, "Delia, no . . ."

And she says, "Save your words for my song, Luther," and gives me another shove, a slap, the slowest of kisses.

Now she sings, a little of "One Night of Sin" and then a bit of "I Can't Be Satisfied." She sings, "Pray God save our souls, Pray God cover our asses," like it's number one on the Pentecostal hit parade. As for her voice, well, it's just what you get when you lace your honey with poison. It's a voice some would kill for, die for, go to the crossroads for. In that voice, I hear sex and midnight. I hear hope, despair, hit songs, and the cure for loneliness. *And the death of us yet*, I think.

So we roll and we tumble, like the old song says. We buck and we wrestle. We fuck and we moan. Delia wants me to fight her, so I fight her, but I'm not much of a fighter. But damn, can I surrender.

And again, again. Once more and again.

The juke-joint band finishes the song, as if on cue. There's applause from the crowd. Whistles and shouts, pleasure chants.

And in the field out back, Delia leans low to whisper into my ear, "It's my band now."

I end up at the bank of a creek, drinking beer and throwing stones. It's not enough of a creek to skip them across; one skip and they thud onto the opposite bank. I let the water nip at the tips of my shoes. My fingertips tingle and some faint voice inside me says, *Delia's right.*

It's her band now. She has the scene in the field to hold over my head, for as long as my head holds any interest for her—for as long as there's a song in there. She'll get her song, of course. And if it's good enough, if it sticks like gum to the country charts, maybe she won't even tell Jimmy Lee about the means to the end. But I'd rather he know, I think. Not because I'm a good person but maybe, a little, because I'd like to be one someday. Maybe because I'd like to do something that never was all that high on the Gaunt list of priorities: sleep at night.

I stand in the doorway of the bar. I watch Jimmy Lee play with the band. They've brought the music down to a low flame now. Delia's sitting at a table in the back corner, long legs crossed, not so much satisfied as triumphant. Buck's glaring at her. If eyes were ice picks . . .

"Your boy ain't bad," Mamie says.

Mamie goes about three hundred pounds; she's heavily made up, with purple eyelids sparkling silver. She's sitting on a barstool by the front door, heavy legs crossed, swinging a high heel from a delicate foot. She has her cigarette holder in one hand and her metal detector in the other.

"Yeah," I say, "natural born."

"Harp player there's mine."

"Good man."

"Nuh-uh, not really. But he's mine."

12

We make it back to the crossroads by two in the morning. There's no sign of the devil. He must have called it a night, or else he's up at the casinos. Delia, seeing the billboards for them, says from the backseat, "Let's play the slots."

"Delia wants to play the slots," Jimmy Lee says.

"Well, it's her band," I say under my breath.

"Jimmy Lee, I fucked your girl."

I'm standing two feet behind Jimmy Lee as he plays the dollar slots. He can't hear a word. He can't hear for the clanging and rattling. He can't hear because of the dead-on focus, the steady concentration, the almost religious fervor required of a casual gambler pissing away his money.

"Jimmy Lee, I fucked Delia, mostly Delia fucked me, we

fucked each other while you played the blues we fucked to, and I am sorry. God, I am one sorry fucker."

I stand there, sighing. My fingertips tingle still. I feel like throwing back my head and yelling, *Can you please shut the fuck up so I can end a friendship and kill a band and we can all get on with it?*

And Jimmy Lee's shouting, "Hot shit, buddy!" as his slot spits out coins. Sounds like it's raining horseshoes.

I wander. I'm handed a drink and drink it down. I turn a corner, minding my own, and nearly run into a girl with a drink tray. She's numb and pretty, showing lots of skin. I say I'm sorry, take another drink, say thank you, drink it down.

I come across Buck. He's sitting at a table, perusing his cards. He's got two fingers of bills in front of him. He's expressionless, Mr. Poker Face. He only nods, takes his cards, and turns cards into money. The dealer frowns, his brow sweats, worried that Buck's about to turn the place back to cotton field.

"Hey, Buck. Did you hear? The band's dead, or will be when Delia decides it's time. It's Delia's band now, see."

The casino has a theme. They all have themes. One's a circus, another is Hollywood. This one is a speakeasy. It's a speakeasy where you can't hear yourself drink, for all the rattling and clanging.

I go looking for a quiet corner, or another numb, pretty girl with a tray of drinks. This time, I'll take them all, swallow them whole, glass and all, in the grand tradition of my daddy, who, it should be noted, worked solo.

I look at the ceiling. I feel a hand in my pocket, fishing.

"Hey, Luth the Truth," Delia says. "Gimme some."

Delia takes two twenties, a few crumpled singles. She puts her face to mine, says, "How about a kiss for the leader of the band?"

"I'm going to tell Jimmy Lee. Soon as things drop to a low roar. Confess all. Take my lumps. Then that'll be that."

"No," she says. "No, you won't. You're a coward that way. You won't say a word. You'll go along, try to get along. The band will stay together, you'll write my song, and then I'll take it from there. Call me what you will, but that's the way it's going to be. Call me what you will, but you're a coward and you fucked your best friend's girl and what's that make you?"

She leaves before she gets her kiss. She leaves before she gets her answer, the answer being, *A ball off my daddy's chain, apparently. And his daddy's, too.*

I end up outside in the parking lot, sitting on the hood of the Merc with the old Cassandra guitar. I run a hand up and down her neck, a finger down and around her curves. But Cassie's having none of me. The gold flowers seem about to wilt in their old age. All is quiet in that dark hollow within.

Sometimes, I think, *it's like she knows.*

I'm not Malcolm, who strung her with his own wild hairs. Malcolm, who stroked and strummed her. I'm not Malcolm, in love and lust and cahoots with her. Malcolm, who could coax from her any sort of song or sound, holy rave-up or drinking chant.

I'm not my daddy, who took her and shook. Together, they rang out with sounds new and old. They whined and moaned, clucked and sputtered. They sounded like those trains, like chickens, like bedsprings and battlefields.

She knows. I'm not my daddy or my daddy's daddy. She can read my doubting mind and my torn heart and the slightest pause in my tingling fingertips. It's not like a Gaunt man to feel guilt or remorse. It's not the Gaunt way.

The guitar seems to play itself. I sing along:

> "*I don't ache for your touch*
> *I just don't care that much*
> *I don't quake*
> *I don't quiver*
> *I don't swoon*
> *I don't melt*
> *when you walk in the room*"

The song drags and plods, sounds like the saddest song ever sung. Not even Nashville with all its polish could save it. I feel sadder still when I'm done. I feel worse, if that's possible—a new low.

It's nice, still and all, when the music moves you.

I'm sitting on the roof of the car when they straggle out. Dawn soon. Delia has a white plastic cup full of quarters. Buck's got bills spilling from his pockets and a grin about to split his face. Jimmy Lee's face is bright as headlights on high beam.

"How much you win?" I say.

"Hundreds, a thou or two," Jimmy Lee says. "Studio time. Recording time. Payola."

He takes Delia in his arms and they spin. Buck jumps and kicks his heels.

"Memphis, then?" I say.

"Memphis," Jimmy Lee says.

PART IV

Pilgrims

1

Memphis at dawn.

First we see the flame. We're all thinking it, but Jimmy Lee, coming out of a road stupor, says it: "The eternal flame?"

But no, it's not Elvis and that's not Graceland. It's an oil refinery on the city's industrial western edge. It's a nice touch, though. It seems to rouse Buck. He'd been drifting those last few miles. Now he sits up, steps on the gas, and goes.

The road rises before us. We come to the crown and hurtle over the thing, trying for airborne. We're the Choctaw Rocket, seems like, for a second there. And then we see it, big and wide and muddy: the Mississippi, the Old Man, the source and wellspring for Saturday night and Sunday morning alike, for my daddy's daddy and my daddy and his son.

"Well, God forbid and holy hell," I say. "Memphis."

2

You can have the ocean. More of a river man, myself. We had a little one, back home. I could stand at the top of the hill and see it, but only in winter. In the summer, the leaves of trees reduced it to a memory, a rumor, and I threw myself down the hill to find it, skidding and sliding, practically falling. I'd grip one tree and then another. It was like flying, like swinging through those trees, but I was grounded as ever.

I'd crouch at the river's edge, lay my hand on the water, tree bark washing away like bits of weathered skin, shedding me. The river was called the Little Riddle. The Little Riddle unravels into the Susquehanna, which spills into the Atlantic Ocean.

I know that now. When I was little, I used to think the Little Riddle was at my beck and prayer. I used to think it went south, to the source of all that drew my daddy. I used to think it would take me to him.

Has it?

The road into Memphis dips and curves and falls in with the river. There's a park between the river and the road. The road is Riverside Drive. The park is named for a black man who long ago saved a slew of white people from drowning as their boat sank in the river. The man was Tom Lee, who couldn't swim but had a little boat. Tom Lee, who didn't tame the river but won a round with it. I read about him on a marker in the park.

We've stopped to stare, we've stopped to piss, we've stopped to stretch. We've stopped because we're in a strange, new place that must be named. And so: home.

"More of an ocean girl, myself," Delia says.

We cross the park. Rocks line the bluff down to the river. Jimmy Lee and Buck try for a closer look. Delia and I stand and watch them go. We stand and watch the river flow. I try to take in its length.

"Delia?"

"Yeah, Luther?"

"What makes you think I can write that song? You've heard my stuff. You know where I stand on the whole Nashville hit-making machine. You know my head's not into that shit and my heart's damn sure not."

"You've written it already, is what I figure."

"Well, that's just you, thinking you know what's what."

"But that's all right. I don't need it yet. I'll tell you when, or you'll just know, one."

"You may think I owe you—"

"You say *owe* or *own*?"

"—but you're sorely—"

"It's like this, Luther. You're smart and clever and haunted and cursed even, I guess. And you're full of guilt and angst. Before your people converted to heathen, I guess they were Catholics. You're all those things at once, and a coward, too. All that stuff, mixed up together—that's where your songs come from. They don't come from that damn guitar. They're inside you. They come out right nice. I like them. I even believe them. I believe you. I believe *in* you. Not as the man for me, I don't mean. As my songwriter. Anyway, you're all I've got at the moment. Let's face it, Luth, Jimmy Lee loses most of his, um, depth when you get above the waist."

She turns to me, puts her hand in my back pocket. "But we're talking about you," she says, "your songs. Yeah, they're rough, some. But they aim to be. That's fine. You know what the river does to a rock? Smoothes it into a stone. A river's good for that much, anyway. And that's what my voice can do to your songs." She leans in to me. "As for any dirty words, well, we can just swap out those silly little fuckers." Her tongue is about in my ear now, hand in my front pocket, and Jimmy Lee is standing at the bank of the Mississippi, trying to skip a stone clear across to Arkansas. "The hook's the thing, you know, and your hooks sink in deep. Little ragged, but we can smooth them, too. We can smooth and we can polish. Spit-shine. Shit, Luth, it goes on every day. It's business."

"Just business."

"You were under the impression, Luther Gaunt, it was ever about anything else with us?"

I find a pay phone with a view of the river. I call my ma.

She tells me she's been reading books about famous musicians. She says they all end the same way. The plane always crashes. Or the car does. Or else the singer drinks himself to death. Or it's pills or the needle. It's always one sort of crash or another.

"Jesus, Ma." But hell, I'm the one who dreams of Patsy Cline's splintered cheekbones and Otis Redding's charred flesh and Buddy Holly's smashed glasses.

"It's okay, Luther. There's got to be some bad, for it to be a good story. Conflict, they call it."

"You're right about that, Ma."

"So how's your story going, Luther?"

"It's going. It's got some of that conflict you mentioned. Enough to keep it interesting, I guess."

"Where are you these days?"

I don't say anything. I just sort of drift, fall in with the flow of the river.

"Luther, you still there?"

"Oh, yeah, Ma. I sure am."

"So where's *there*?"

"Memphis, you know."

"I didn't know, but I might have guessed."

"We just got here. I'm standing here looking at the river. It's big and muddy, all right. I guess it didn't get that name anywhere strange."

"It's always looked that way, from the pictures."

"There's a barge going by. Arkansas on the other side. Memphis, it's over my shoulder, sitting on the bluff. I wonder . . ."

I wonder if my daddy is up there somewhere. I stop myself. I think she might fill the dead air, but no.

"You still there, Ma?"

"Oh, yeah, Luther. I'm here."

3

The old man answers the phone on the seventh ring, a weary voice saying, "Yeah, what?" like that's the name of the joint and it's closing time.

"Is Doc there? Doc Wise?" I've called the phone number Jimmy Lee never got around to calling, that day he first saw Delia. This Doc Wise is supposed to be a bar owner in need of a regular band.

"Speaking."

"Well, my name's—"

"Hold on a sec."

I hear the sound of a glass being fetched and filled, a deep voice not Doc's saying, "Same ol', same ol'." I hear faint jukebox sound but can't make out the song.

"Yeah?"

"Me, you mean?" I say.

"Yeah, you were about to say your name."

"Luther Gaunt. And, well—"

"Gaunt, you say." Was that a catch in his voice? The slightest pause?

"Yeah, well—"

"Let me guess. You've got a band and you want to play here, in my bar. Let's us see. I figure you're the singer, though you seem kinda shy, just talking to you on the phone, can barely get you to say shit. But yeah, you're the singer, I figure. Frontman."

"So we're called—"

"Let me guess. Well, you ain't the Memphis Jug Band or Cannon's Jug Stompers or the Mississippi Sheiks. You ain't the Delta Cats or the Kings of Rhythm. You ain't the . . . no, I reckon you ain't the Blue Flames either." Doc Wise seems to be warming to his own curmudgeon's lament. "You wouldn't be the Mar-Keys or the Bar-Kays? No, I don't guess. And you sure as hell ain't Booker T. & The MGs. Sure as shit ain't Big Star." He sighs, seems about to say more, but . . .

"You know, there's still some good music being written these days. And not every good band name's been taken."

"What're you boys called?"

"Um, the Long Gone Daddies."

Old Doc Wise seems about to cackle. "Well, that's original!"

"Yeah, well, you know. We love the old stuff. We just play our version of it. Wondering maybe could we play it in your bar? All those old Jug Stompers being dead and gone, pretty much."

"Reckon I better give a listen, then."

4

I remember those old pictures of Colonel Tom Parker—the big, bald head, giant and misshapen, like something the neighbor's garden grew. Folks would come from miles around to see. "Holy shit, Mabel!" they'd say. It would've won the blue ribbon at the state fair, except no one could say what it was, exactly.

But don't mind me. I'm just not much of a fan of the man. Tom Parker, that old carny, came and stole Elvis's soul and turned him into a movie prop.

I have this mental image of Doc Wise as Colonel Tom Parker—a dirty, low thief out to steal our swagger, our souls.

My daddy told me one time about a dream he'd had. He was at Graceland with Elvis. He was there to pick some guitar with the King. He'd been summoned. John Gaunt wasn't the sort to be summoned, but I figured he went just so he could tell Elvis to his pretty face that Carl Perkins was the higher talent. In the dream, John Gaunt got to Graceland and was shown in. He'd never been there, but he knew something was wrong.

"Elvis stood in the center of the room—the one they call the Jungle Room, you know—and he wondered would the blood come out of the carpet. He didn't seem to be worried so much about that lump on the floor. Colonel Tom Parker could be hauled out with the trash. But blood was oozing from his wound, blood was dripping from the blade, all of it was seeping into the carpet, and that was Elvis's carpet, and Elvis liked that carpet, didn't want to have to buy new. 'Oh, Mama,' Elvis said. 'Oh, Mama, please.' Elvis's mama was dead. She'd been dead for years. He missed her still. We all of us get only one mama. He shook his head, seemed about to cry. But then he righted himself. He looked at that lump on the floor. He smiled a smile that all but steamed the blood from the carpet of the Jungle Room, you know. All but. And then he took some pills and . . ."

My daddy would stop his stories in mid-sentence, but I took all I could from them. I memorized them. I hoarded them, burned them into my mind. I gobbled my daddy's words like they were Elvis's pills.

There was more to this one, though. It didn't come for another four, five months. The next time my daddy was home from the road, he said, "I had that dream again, Luther. Or anyway, I had more of it. Colonel Tom Parker had been hauled to the sidewalk outside the Graceland gates, and good goddamn for him. Then me and Elvis, we sat down in what they call the Jungle Room, you know, and started to pick our guitars. He wanted to try the old Cassandra and I let him. He wasn't but a rudimentary picker, but Cassie can bring stuff out of a man that's not even there. I played a black electric, a Gibson. It was sleek and loud and I liked the feel of it. I felt like I was cheating on Cassie. But hell, she was over there in Elvis's arms. So I played that sleek electric one. Boy, did I. About the best I played, ever. I shook the carpet from the ceiling.

"Well, Elvis, he played rhythm and I played lead, but I let him sing. We played old rockers and gospel tunes, classic country, and Lord, we played some blues. We played through the night and finally, along about dawn, I said I'd better hit it. Elvis walked me to the door, said, 'Thanks for coming by, John Gaunt.' He said he liked my playing and I said I liked his singing. I did, too. I didn't even bring up Carl Perkins. Just wasn't, you know, the time.

"Well, I turned to walk away, but I could tell he wanted to say something else. I stopped. He said, 'I ought to feel free now, but I don't, John. What if I leave and you stay here?' I said, 'You want to give me Graceland?' 'Yeah,' he said. 'Trade it straight up for that old Cassandra Special Rider guitar.' I just turned and kept walking down the driveway there at Graceland. I said over my shoulder, 'It's been a long day and a longer night, Elvis. You've killed the Colonel dead and dumped him on the sidewalk with the garbage. But now you're talking crazy.'"

Doc Wise is a live ringer for the Colonel.

Or maybe that's just the way I see it through my eyes, clouded with road dust, guilt, shame, remorse. He leans on the bar, nods as we carry in our instruments. I feel mean and nervous and don't say a word.

Once we're set up, I count off and start singing. I beat on the old guitar like I need to wake my granddaddy and tell him something vital to us both. Cassie warms to me and that old Gaunt abandon. Jimmy Lee's right there with me, spewing notes like alley slurs. We play "Elvis '53" and then rip into our version of rockabilly:

I got a girl
she's willing and able
she can drink Memphis
under the table

I got a girl
I just let her be
she walks around naked
saying the rosary

I lunge and stomp as Jimmy Lee makes his guitar sound like a hundred whips cracking. Buck's drums sound like echoes of outlaw gunplay across the flat Southland. Delia stands back and to the side, giving a reasonable approximation of amateur bass playing.

The room moves in a blur around us. I see glimpses of paintings on yellow walls, brown hoodoo women, bands of musicians, silken guitar strings, gold, curvaceous horns.

We grab the songs by their tails like jungle cats and whip them around our heads. We slow them to a stroll, soothing the beasts. We play all of our originals. We let the room grow quiet, then I sort of half-sing, half-talk as Jimmy Lee picks a delicate blues, fingers on strings like picking a lock:

I play hell
just to get to you
I say penance
when we're through
I put it all in a song
did I get to you?

And we're off again, Jimmy Lee playing a swampy guitar, all thick with undergrowth, the kind you come upon sometimes in storybooks. There's usually a dead body in there, if it's that kind of story, that kind of book. Then Jimmy Lee pulls back, plays one shocking blue note; it's as if he's just seen that dead body and recognized it as a dear friend. He turns to me, winks and grins as he does, awash in the wonder that is Jimmy Lee Vine with a guitar in his hands and the stage at his feet. This not being a good time to talk of backstabbing and double-crossing him, I go into the one about Buddy Holly's spectacles.

The floor is hot to the touch when we finish. We stand, triumphant gods, arms crossed, looking at Doc Wise, who's come out from behind the bar and is walking toward us. He's fat and he waddles. I think for a second that he's these things in a lovable sort of way. I think he's about to break into a smile. I forget for a moment the man's likeness—real or imagined—to Tom Parker. Say what you will, but the Colonel was shrewd; the man could turn dust to money.

Hell, I want to be discovered.

Doc Wise says only, "Does the girl sing?"

So Delia sings "One Night of Sin," knocks that fat cretin of a Colonel Tom Parker knockoff flat on his wallet. We get the gig, and big fucking deal about that, okay?

5

"**Y**ou're still the lead singer," Delia says. "You're still Luth the Truth, one and only voice of the Long Gone Daddies. I'll just, you know, come on for a few songs a night."

We're having a Memphis-style Sunday brunch at the Furry Dice, Doc Wise's bar: beer and barbecue sandwiches. We also seem to be having some sort of meeting, though only Delia is talking.

Then Jimmy Lee says, as if he's been deputized, "That's right, Luth."

Buck shrugs. Buck seems preoccupied with that barbecue sandwich. It takes two hands to hold and it's dripping sauce. It seems to have a mound of slaw on it. He seems in awe.

I lean back and take a drink of beer. It's good and cold and crisp, though the label smells of cigarettes. I take a pack from my pocket and shake one out. I light it and look at Delia through the smoke. I can see clear through the haze to those blue eyes and the spinning wheels behind. And I have a vision most frightening: Colonel Tom Parker as a bombshell dirty blonde with a voice of honey and a heart of trickery.

"But," Delia says, "you saw what closed the deal. You heard what the man said. So we'll just, you know, play it by ear."

Buck is lost in that pig-meat sandwich, gone to the smoked glory of it. Jimmy Lee considers what Delia said and shakes his head for the longest time, searching for a word, but it's as if wiser men have made off with them all. "Well," he says.

"So I guess there's no point bringing it to a vote, then," I say.

Delia and Jimmy Lee leave for Graceland in the Merc. Buck just leaves.

Which leaves me on a wobbly stool at the bar, listening to the hum of the air conditioner and the radio. It's not one of the commercial stations. It's not a smooth voice that's talking. You can hear today's cigarettes and last night's whiskey, the crust and varnish of life, too much fucking life. The voice says the station is WEVL and the show is called *The Memphis Shakedown*. Then the guy starts to play a record—a real record, scratches and all—and it's Johnny Cash and the Tennessee Two, "Hey Porter," and that one sounds so good he plays another, "Train of Love," and I think, *I'm with that, I love a good train song. The national anthem ought to be a good train song. Are there any other kinds of train songs?* And that's all the DJ does, is play records. Then he talks a little about the records. He says Johnny wrote "Hey Porter" when he was in the army, stationed in Germany. *Tell me something I don't know*, says me to myself, and the DJ says, like I'm there beside him, that Johnny wore black because that's the only color he and the Tennessee Two could find in matching outfits. Which I did not know.

So I sit and drink and listen, bucked up a little despite the state of the band, as the DJ plays one old, beautiful song after another, no commercials, just his little bits about the songs and the occasional public-service announcement about not leaving dogs in cars with the windows up in the high heat of summer while you're inside the store shopping for groceries, and hey, I'm with that, too, I like dogs. And then the DJ plays one by Carl Perkins, "Matchbox." Well, fuck me in my prime. Much better now. Music for this boy's soul, beer for his belly. I've found a way, however temporary, to bypass my heart and head altogether.

"I used to have a show on that station," Doc Wise says now.

He's standing over me, swapping out beers. I get a better look. The Colonel Parker resemblance is fading. His face just looks tired, worn, and faded. Big and round but starting to deflate.

"Oh, yeah?"

"Yeah. Few years ago, back when I, you know, believed in things and music."

"What'd you play?"

"Murder ballads, mostly. Show was called *These Blues Are Killing Me*. I don't know. I started listening too close to my own songs. One day, I had a breakdown on the air. I don't mind telling you this—you mind hearing it?"

I must look like a fellow lodge brother in the fuckup club. Must be just stamped on my damn forehead. I give a nod.

"Well, things weren't going good with the wife," he says. "She was stepping out. I thought she was. Songs I played, the wife was always stepping out. Or the husband was. Or they both were. But I was always here, slinging drinks. So I got suspicious, got jealous, and my mind got all hopped up on the idea she was going to have me killed. Hired job, you know. Well, I ran with that one. I imagined she'd given him the time and place to do the job. It would be during my radio show. My show didn't start until two in the morning, Monday nights, after I finished up here. The radio station would be deserted then, the neighborhood would be. The station's in a building on the fringe of downtown, you see, just like the station is on the fringe of the dial. It just works out that way. It's a volunteer station. The DJs play their record collections, you know. They do it because they love the music, is all. You with me, young Luther Gaunt?"

"I'm with you, Doc," I say.

And Doc says, "So anyway, she wanted to know the moment it happened. She wanted to hear it live on the radio, in the middle of introducing one of my songs. She hated that music. She fucking despised it. Her name was Dorothy. I hate that name, Dorothy. Wouldn't let me call her Dottie or Dot, and fine with me—I didn't want to. Anyway, the guy she hired, well, he would steal into the station, plug me in the back just as I was introducing one of my murder ballads. I had all this worked out. Had it planned. It was like a movie, what they call cinematic."

He pauses, but not for effect or my two cents. I think he's just watching that picture show. He smiles, but just a little. He says, "Well, in my head, the hired gun sits outside the station with his car window down, key in the ignition, radio on. He's listening to my show. He's bored at first. This is just another job. He once thought he was above this. He was born too late. He wanted to be an outlaw on horseback, robbing banks in broad daylight and riding away, I don't know, into folklore. There was nothing heroic about this job. He didn't know me. He didn't particularly like my wife. Which figures—he'd, you know, met her. Fact is, he hated her, the vile, cheating wife. He'd had one of them. He'd had a couple.

"So he sits and listens to my show. Those old tales of guns and knives, hate and revenge and love gone deep south. They pull him in. They do that to a fella. So the time of the hit comes and goes. He decides to let me live as long as I play great songs. The first sour note I sound, I'm dead. It becomes a game with him. With me, too. So I keep spinning these little stays of execution. He knows I know and I know he knows I know. He's judge and jury. I could live with that. I play another, and another. I play the one about the banks of the Ohio, and the one about Pretty Polly. All those old ones. By the end of the night, there's a considerable body count. My songs are full of dead husbands, dead wives, children, strangers, runaways, prison breakers, gamblers, pimps, lawmen, decent folk who got in the way. But I live. I'm spared.

"But next week, he's back, and the week after. And so that's how I did my show every week. Until, I don't know, I got tired of waiting. My wife, she ran off. I guess I never was important enough to have shot. Her name was Dorothy, a name I despise. Did I mention that?"

I shake my head. I take a drink of beer, breathe in the cigarette fumes from the label. I say, "Yeah, I believe you let that slip, Mr. Doc Wise."

He says, "So one night, I just broke down. Fell apart on the air. I think I played that song about Stagger Lee and that John B. Stetson hat something like seventeen times straight before they came for me. I was hospitalized for, as they say, observation." He breathes deep, puts his hands on his hips. "I'm better now. I'm okay. I got most of my wise-ass back. I got a woman I see sometimes. She's mean as me. I like a woman with some fight. Say, you want another beer?"

"I could do with another."

"You boys do any murder ballads?"

"Nope, not really. My songs all have metal detectors, seems like. No guns allowed. Some might call it a weakness, but I like to think things might work out somehow for the people in my songs. Oh, they get stewed and they screw around and they sure fuck up, but usually not in any way fatal. They get to live. They get to try again."

Doc smiles and says, "Oh, you like to really punish 'em."

"Yeah, well," I say. "And you—you believe a song can save your life."

"Well, I used to."

"I still do," I say. And then, "So what did you really think of us? Just the core band, you know. Not the girl."

"Kind of hard to separate, now, ain't it, Luther Gaunt?" he says, rubbing the crown of his bald head. "I mean, once you've seen and heard her."

He doesn't mean anything by it. It's the truth, only.

There being nothing to add to that, I pay the man and don't hold anything against him. I say we'll see him tomorrow night. Tomorrow is the last day of July.

"Don't forget to bring the girl!" he shouts as the door shuts.

Doc Wise's story sounds like one my daddy would have told me. I wonder, though, would he have gone for something as subtle as a nervous breakdown on live radio? Then I wonder what it says about me that I think a nervous breakdown is a subtle way to go.

I like the story, though. I don't even wonder if it's true. My rooting interest is in the record. My interest is in the record playing ever on.

Believe the songs, I say. Put your faith in them.

One of them may just save your life.

6

I walk the streets, gray and abandoned. Warehouses. Empty lots. Fences rimmed with barbed wire.

I stop at the corner of East McLemore and College, the empty lot there. I lean against the stop sign and think, *Okay, here are the facts: The band has made it to Memphis, gotten a bit of a break . . . The band is dying . . . The band is dying and I'm killing it . . . All I feared is coming to pass . . . All I have is the band and the band is dying and I'm killing it . . . No, it's Delia who's killing it. But I'm the accomplice.*

I walk for hours down random streets. I end up at the empty lot where the Stax Records studio once stood—where it stood before it was demolished by a church to make room for something that was never built. Now there's nothing but emptiness and broken glass. And a historical marker at the corner that tells the tale of Stax.

I walk on, across blocks and neighborhoods, past a church, a pawnshop, a church, a pawnshop, a liquor store, a homeless mission. A soul-food restaurant, a fix-it shop. Hairdresser. Record store. Church, pawn, church. I pass a bar but don't go in. I'll try anything once. Then I double back and go inside.

An old, wiry black man cleans a pistol behind the bar while the jukebox plays a Staple Singers song about God in heaven. "Help you, son?" he says without looking up.

I'm the only customer in the barroom, but there seems to be some commotion from a back room or beyond. I order a beer and he hands me a bottle. The label smells like cigarettes, like at Doc's place. Must be a Memphis thing.

"Slow day?" I say.

"Nah, not really." He looks at me. His eyes are red-rimmed, cobwebbed. He motions to the back.

"Oh," I say, as if I'm wise to all that.

He lifts his pistol. It shines and gleams like pistols do sometimes. "Like it?"

"Nice one, I guess, as pistols go."

"Got it down to the pawn." The old man is sitting on a silver stool covered with red, ripped fabric. Now he stands and reaches below the bar to a wooden chest with a padlock on it. He unlocks the lock, opens the chest, drops the pistol in with several dozen more, all shining and gleaming.

The jukebox plays another soul song about sweet heaven and then one about funky Mississippi.

"You collect them?"

"Nah, not like that," he says. "Ridding the city of 'em. Forty-two down."

"How many to go?"

"Don't know, don't wanna. Can't count that high, I don't guess. Just count the ones at hand. Forty-one, forty-two. I get higher'n they taught me to go at ol' Manassas High, maybe I quit, maybe I don't." He has a singsong way of talking; it's a little sweet heaven and some funky Mississippi.

He reaches his right hand across the bar. We shake.

"Ike Lyon," he says. "Bartender, ex-preacher, banjo picker."

"Banjo picker, really? Wow. My name's Luther Gaunt, by the way. I sing in a rock 'n' roll band. We just hit town."

"Watch it," he says. "This town'll do you bad. I love it, but it will. This town'll shoot you where you stand and lift your wallet before you fall. God, I love it. Been here all my days. But still and all, still and all . . ."

"Yeah, well, most of our wounds are self-inflicted, seems like."

The door opens and two guys in shades walk past—strut, I guess you'd say. Ike Lyon nods as they go. A door to a back room opens and closes, a clatter rises and falls. Ike shakes his head.

"Card game? Dice?"

"Something."

"Banjo picker," I say again. "What did you play? Do you still?"

"Used to be in a jug band. Played with Cannon's Stompers and them. I wasn't much but a kid. Sixty-odd year ago. Don't play much anymore. Don't play at all, at the moment. Traded my old banjo for that last pistol, number forty-two."

"Damn."

"Can't rid the city of guns with one hand and play the 'Minglewood Blues' with the other'n."

"No, I guess not. Hard enough for me to do one thing at a time. Sometimes, playing my guitar up there on stage, I forget to breathe."

"What kind you play?"

"An old Cassandra Special Rider from the thirties. My daddy played it, and his, too."

"About the color of whiskey, just slightly watered down?"

"That's it."

"Got gold flowers on it?"

"Surely does."

"Oh, fine guitar. Buddy of mine played one in the old jug band. He'd throw a beautiful gal over sooner'd he part with that guitar. Banjo players, they particular about their banjos, but not like that."

"Guitars have those curves, I guess is the thing about them."

"Must be it, those curves. You call her by name?"

"Cassie."

"I never did call my banjo anything particular. I miss it, still and all."

He slides another beer my way.

"Thanks, Mr. Ike Lyon." And then, "How much would it take to get it out of pawn?"

"I could get it for a song," he says, smiling. "Not much call for banjos these days. Not in this neighborhood. Don't know about yours. Guy at the pawn just being kindly to a crazy old man. Trading a gun for a banjo in this neighborhood ain't a good way to stay in the pawn business. I tell him, I say, 'God be watching and God be smiling down upon you, son.' He say, 'God got His eye on that banjo, He can have it and cheap, old man.' "

I grin. I have a mental picture of the Supreme Being picking an old four-string, playing the "Minglewood Blues."

"Are you a God-fearing man?" Ike Lyon says.

I haven't been asked this for some time. I never knew what to say when my grandmother Sara Gaunt asked me. But now the answer just comes to me.

"I don't think that's what God has in mind."

The old man drops his head as if to think this over, scratches the scruff of his chin.

"Fair enough, young man," he says finally. "Good answer."

Then there's a faraway crack of gunfire. Ike Lyon lifts his head, holds it still.

"Three blocks away and moving this way," he says, as if he's tracking a storm, counting the seconds between the thunderclaps. "Might want to hoof it, son," he says, and I do.

I walk on. On I walk. Near downtown, I tire of walking and hail a cab.

"Where the foot of Beale dips a toe into the mighty Mississippi, good man." I'd wanted to say it, just like that, forever.

The cabbie says, "Hell, son, just keep walking the way you walking, you be wet in no time and drowned in five minutes more."

And so I walk on. On I walk, to the river. I sit and watch it flow as daylight goes to dusk. The river seems almost gray in this light, a shining metal, shade of a gun barrel after Mr. Ike Lyon, barkeep, ex-preacher, banjo picker, gets his gentle hands on it. He had long, thin fingers, his skin giving his bones only cursory cover. I bet he could play the hell out of the banjo. I bet he could play the heaven out of it.

I walk toward our dive hotel downtown. I hike and hoof it. I don't come across a soul, just this old guy in a lemon-yellow cowboy suit who wants to give me his car. It's a long stretch of shiny, black Caddy and he says it just brings him down, the color.

"I already have a car," I say.

"What color?"

"Muddy brown."

"Now *that's* uplifting."

"No thanks, just the same."

The man in the lemon-yellow suit reaches into the car and pulls out a lemon-yellow cowboy hat. He's wearing a white shirt and all I can think of is meringue. He puts on the hat. He's tall, wide, and white-haired; a nub of a cigarette pokes from his mouth like mutant stubble. He reaches in his car again and pulls out a guitar. He rakes his thick, stubby fingers across the strings.

"I'm doing what Elvis done," he says.

"Giving away cars?"

"Yep."

I say, "Elvis didn't give them away because he didn't like the color. He gave them away because he had a big heart."

"That's what killed him, his big heart. His big heart just give out."

"I think it was Colonel Tom Parker who killed him, in a manner of speaking. That's what I think."

He considers this theory of mine. He says, "Well, maybe you right about that, brother."

We shake on it.

"Ronnie Dale Crown," he says, "from down at East Palatka, Florida. Quit my job in the furniture showroom just Monday week, reached deep into my closet and pulled out this suit, says to the wife, 'Wife, I'm gonna give it one more good goddamn try.' Music, I mean. I sing country. Got in this car and nosed it toward Nashville."

"Uh, Ronnie Dale, this is Memphis."

"I overshot it," he says, his grin giving way to a huge, open-mouth laugh that resounds down the empty street.

He reaches into his car one more time and pulls out a couple of beers. We sit on the hood of that long stretch of shiny, black Caddy, and we drink. It's parked in the middle of a street called South Main, lined by boarded-up storefronts. A few are being refurbished. There's some new paint being splashed around, scaffolding in place. Urban renewal is coming, but it's not here yet.

"My name's Luther Gaunt. Lead singer and songwriter for

the Long Gone Daddies. I'm most pleased to come across you and your beer, Ronnie Dale Crown."

He pats my back like he was some boy's daddy, once upon a long gone day. "Say, Luther, we in the same business."

"How's that business?"

"Been better," he says, grinning again. "I seem to be an . . . what's the word? Uh-nack-row-nism. Man out of place and time. But I figure I'll stay awhiles. Something about this place makes me want to, you know. Must be all these ghosts around. Figure I'll walk the streets Elvis and them boys walked. Sop up that history. Maybe get a song out of it, you know."

"I know."

"Or maybe it's just one big ol' excuse to wear this yeller suit."

I don't say Ronnie Dale might have better professional luck if he gave away the suit instead of the car. Then I go ahead and say it and I pat his back, like I was some man's son, once upon a long gone day.

We crack another round of beers as night falls. Nobody ever does show up, not even a cop to ask what the hell we think we're doing in the middle of South Main Street, Memphis, Tennessee, drunk and hooting, pining for ghosts.

I leave when the beer runs out. The last sight I see is Ronnie Dale Crown standing on his hood strumming his guitar, singing an old country weeper about an old country singer who sings nothing but country weepers and can't catch a break, not even one.

Ronnie Dale is sixty if he's a day, has a voice like a cat fight. I like him. He's an anachronism, a man out of time and place. Which is to say he wears his lemon-yellow cowboy suit on days other than Halloween.

He's still playing as I walk out of sight, out of earshot, and turn the corner to the hotel. Delia, Jimmy Lee, and Buck are walking out the front door. They say they're going to drink Beale Street dry and ask do I want to come along.

"No."

But I find myself falling in with them.

Beale, that long-dead street of schemes, where liquor flowed and bullets flew and pretty women dressed to the glittering nines and sang songs and showed endless leg and maybe swooned a little, if swooning was in that year, and men shook dice, fired shots and drank them, chased the aforementioned pretty women in their glittering nines—that Beale, the Beale of old, the Beale of dirty minds, low-down blues, and other cures for what-all ails you, has been tidied up and tamed, strung up by a short leash and turned into a tourist-beckoning, two-block strip of night-clubs: bourbon renewal.

We pour into a little slip of a bar called Blues Hall, find a round, rickety table in the back, beers all around. A band is play-ing a tame version of "The Thrill Is Gone," looking for a way in-side the song.

The band is pale and reverent; the song won't let them in. Suddenly, they stop in something resembling unison. The lead singer, a fresh-scrubbed, flat-topped redhead, says in a British accent, "We're taking a little break now. See you blokes in a few."

Jimmy Lee yells at the singer, "Bloke you!"

"They could use a new singer," Delia says.

"Good Lord," I say. "Haven't you done enough, woman?"

Delia's wearing a little pink Elvis T-shirt she bought at Grace-land, black leather pants, black shoes with ice-pick heels. It's like this: I can't stand to look and I can't help but stare. In my stare are hate, envy, lust, and many beers.

"So how much of a hoot was Graceland?" I say. I plan to go

later on my own, the lone-pilgrim act.

"Tastefully appointed," Jimmy Lee says. Which, you know, you don't often hear about Graceland.

As for Delia, she liked seeing all of the gold and platinum records.

As we talk, a brittle, old black man ambles onto the stage carrying a cane chair and a scuffed guitar that looks like something the pawnshop threw out. He sits down, drops his head so that all we see is the top of it, dark and rippled with a patch of gray scruff. His hands fall to the strings, but he doesn't play a note. The old man looks like an exhibit in a museum of blues history, except that the museum seems to have lost its funding and the exhibit has gone to dust and tatters.

Now one foot taps a steady beat. He begins to pull at the strings and the old guitar rings, it chimes, and the old man sings a blues that's more feeling than words, his scratchy, old caw of a voice making sounds that leave language fumbling for something to say. Even Delia inches to the edge of her seat to watch.

It goes on like that for five minutes, ten. Then it ends. He stands, takes his leave amid stunned applause, and out the door he walks, a ghost of a ghost. To this day, I don't know if it really happened.

The Brits watch from against the back wall. They huddle before they return to the stage. When they start playing again, they've abandoned their reverence and the copped licks. They're playing *their* version of the blues—punked up, ugly and raw, but joyous. Joyous because it's theirs and it's them. The singer is particularly demonic, has a voice that makes you cover your ears and order double scotches. They play for forty minutes, then flame out, all but collapsing. It takes a lot out of a guy, inventing a whole new you. It takes even more, becoming yourself.

The singer reaches once more for the microphone, slowly,

woozily, as if he's thinking of asking it to do more than dance with him.

"Good night, Memphis. Our name's Bunk. Leaving now. Got a long crawl home."

Bunk—like what happens when punk rides the blues like a train. I smile.

The next night, it's the Long Gone Daddies on the stage of the Furry Dice before a small but rapt audience of drunks and strays. They're a thirsty lot, at any rate.

At one point, I look up from a song to see Doc Wise actually smile. I wonder, does the old man, in this small moment, believe again in music and things? Does he believe one of our songs can save his life?

Delia comes on just before the break to sing "One Night of Sin." She has it down now. She owns the song. She owns the crowd, such as it is. It'll be bigger. Word of mouth. Word of mouth with dropped jaw.

It's just the one song she sings the first night.

The next night, she also sings backup on three of my originals.

The night after that, we duet on "Elvis '53."

She's been paying attention. She knows the words; she knows the songs. She inhabits them; she moves in and redecorates, changes them to suit her mood, her desires, her plots and plans. She has some of Patsy Cline's phrasing.

Listen closely, though, and you can hear the smoothing process, the commercialization of the heretofore-outcast Long Gone Daddies.

A couple of weeks into our gig at the Furry Dice, there's a bit about us in the local free weekly newspaper—that is to say, there's a bit about Delia, an interview with her. The writer gets around to mentioning the Long Gone Daddies in the third paragraph. Seems we're her "backing band."

Another week and the crowds are out the door and to the rafters and I'm a sideman who stands in the shadows and keeps his mouth shut.

7

Doc Wise slides me a beer across the bar.

"Schlitz," he says. "That was Patsy Cline's brand."

"I didn't know that. But I figured, you know, she had a brand."

"They say she could cuss like a sailor," Doc Wise says. "They say she told dirty jokes that could make the men blush. They say she was tough, because she had to be tough, being a cowgirl singer in a man's world. They say she could cuss a blue streak."

"I'll venture she was cussing a blue streak," I say, "when that little airplane went down."

It's late morning of the latest misplaced day. I've come to see Doc Wise, seeking wisdom. A man with a name like Doc Wise ought to be a deep font of such stuff.

"You wonder why that happens," I say. "Why all those planes go down."

Doc Wise joins me in a drink. He hunches his shoulders, says, "Lots of reasons. Engine failure. Pilot error. Storms, ice, fog. You know, visibility zero."

"No, I mean . . . Well, I mean, why Patsy? Why Otis? Why Buddy, and Ritchie Valens?" I take a drink. I take another. I say, "Oh, I guess it's because the no-name, no-account bands can't afford to fly. They cram into vans—or muddy-brown Mercs—and move on to the next town. And anyway, if they were to fly and they were to perish—*poof*—I guess we might not even hear of it. But still."

Doc Wise leans back, seems to consider whatever it is I'm getting at.

"You think God should take care of them because they're who they are," he says. "They're artists. You think God should . . . what's the word? Intercede. You believe that much in the music?"

"Yeah, well."

"And in God, apparently."

The radio plays "Will Jesus Wash the Bloodstains from Your Hands?" Doc Wise gives the radio a dirty look, says he doesn't like songs that ask questions. He prefers more along the lines of the definitive statement. He says that's what he needs, at this point in life. He says he needs hard truths, even if they're not true.

" 'I Can't Quit You, Baby,' 'I Wanna Be Your Dog'—that sort of thing, you mean?"

Doc smiles and takes a drink of his beer. He says, "I don't know what I mean."

"So much for that deep font of wisdom."

"All anybody gets here is twelve ounces."

And he fetches me another.

"Delia's going to be a star," Doc says finally. "I do know that. I can't say whether she'll like it so much once she is one. My guess is, fame's not all the famous mean it to be. But she's going to be a star. I do know that."

"Well, Doc, you could have kept it to yourself."

Another night and we're back on stage. I have vague notions of sabotage, foul play, of playing nothing but the riff from "I Wanna Be Your Dog."

The moment arrives, but not the nerve. My nerve is lying especially low these days.

So I shout some backup vocals and strum the old Cassandra and watch my boots and a drunk girl in the fifth row and the pressed-tin ceiling and the slow turn of ceiling fans, anything to avoid looking at Delia. And then I look at Delia.

She's blue-jeaned and barefoot tonight. She's wearing an old, gray filling-station shirt she bought at a local thrift store. The name stitched on the shirt is Luther. She has her usual disregard for buttons. She's a head taller than the rest of us, out on the edge of the stage. What do they call that? Perspective? She's leaning over the edge, singing a slow one, pleading, her voice now down to a whisper; it's the loudest sound in the bar.

Now the cheers, hoots, and hollers, louder than I've heard in all my barroom days, louder than should be possible for a place the size of the Furry Dice.

Delia says, "That's all for me, y'all. Luther—that's him in the shadows there—he'll take you on home from here."

She turns to me. I meet her at the microphone, look up into her eyes, and see that perspective can defy mere fact. Perspective is a ton of bricks, a piano, that some people drop on some others.

So Delia has risen to her moment and taken it. I've run from mine, slumped in the shadows. She leans down, seeming

two heads taller now in her bare feet, takes my hand inside that
filling-station shirt for quite a damn feel, just as quickly takes
my hand away. She kisses my forehead and says, "That's a little
something for you, Luther boy."

"And what about all those people out there, Delia, worked up
as they are?" I say. "What about them?"

"Damn, but you know nothing about being a star. You ain't
got the foggiest. You don't leave yourself spent on the floor. You
walk out tall with something left. You leave them wanting. You
leave them wanting the only thing a star has to sell."

"What's that, Delia?"

"The promise of more."

Now she's gone, like how the stars do it, and I'm standing
there in the wake of her, in the want of more.

I sit in a chair on the stage, head down and hunkered. I start
to strum. I try to tune out the sight and sound of a bar emptying.
I'm a one-man police raid, but that's fine. This one's for me and
the six people somewhere in this world who get tired of craning
their necks at shooting stars and other stellar wonders, who get
tired of looking at some damn place they'll never get to go.

"You can write songs on the river bottom, too," I say without
looking up.

"I been there, brother!" a drunk shouts.

I play one of my old ones. I play it haltingly, an uphill country
waltz:

> Well, I take mercy
> and you take leave
> of your senses
> I believe
> you'll dance
> while I grieve

Here's my heart
where's your sleeve?

Down on the river bottom, I dig in. I try for deeper still. I play every sad song I can conjure. I play "I Wanna Be Your Dog" as a dirge. I go half an hour into the broken heart of busted hopes. Slowly, I come out of it. I start to bang away on the old Cassandra, as if to bust it into splinters. I thump the body, pound the strings. I stand and stomp. The chair goes flying.

Wake up Sunday morning
with your Saturday-night pain
walk all the way to Monday
lean on your Tuesday cane
Wednesday don't deny me
Thursday don't change your name
Friday fetch my bottle
Let's do it
do it
do it
do it again

Sunday morning's at the mirror
Saturday night's doin' time
Monday's called in sickly
Tuesday's ass is mine
Wednesday had a notion
but Thursday robbed it blind
Friday grab my pistol
Let's do it
do it
do it
one last time

Let's do it
do it
do it
for old times

I spit words and venom. I pour menace, chase it with rage. I've come undone, unglued, unhinged. I've come within a hair trigger of smashing Cassie on the stage. I fall to the stage without as much as a shove, and then . . .

I smash that old Cassandra guitar to splinters, bust family history to bits and pieces and gold petals of pretty flying flowers.

8

Two days later.
    I'm sitting in my hotel room. I'm finishing the song. I'm putting the words and music down on paper, for Delia and posterity. I hear her singing in my head as I write. I hear the music. I hear the song as a polished stone. Maybe, just maybe, it's a gem. Maybe fool's platinum. I hear Delia's voice—honed to perfection by studio gimmicks and thirteen takes—take the song just where she wants it to go.

I usually fancy my songs as stones to throw—across creeks, through windows—but this one seems to have a flight plan of its own. It floats and flutters, does its own thing, and doesn't care one whit if I claim it. It doesn't seem to think I have much claim upon it.

The door opens and in she walks. Delia in a black dress—the national flag of deceit, flying about half-staff—and those ice-pick heels. Delia, Delia, Delia. She doesn't say a word, just lies on her back on the bed, stretching out, head on a pillow, watching me finish.

She's come for the song and I take it to her. I kiss circles around her ankles—such thin, delicate things they are, women's ankles, strange marvels of engineering, making no sense whatsoever, quivering when they walk in ice-pick heels. She's come for the song and I whisper the words to her gilded calves, to first one knee, then the other. I part her legs, kiss her rose tattoo.

> *"I don't ache for your touch*
> *I just don't care that much"*

My face disappears into her and my mind goes blank. No, not blank. My mind has the answer for a particular question I've always had: What's it like to drive a car over a cliff to the nothingness below? To not think too much, to not worry at all? To give yourself over to the ride? What's that like?

Just as I always suspected, it is exhilaration and ecstasy and it is utter freedom, for as long as it lasts. It seems as if it will last forever.

Remorse and shame won't take that ride. They stop at the edge of the cliff, shake their heads, and wag their fingers.

The nothingness below, hell's scrap heap, awaits.

> *"I don't quiver*
> *I don't quake*
> *I don't swoon"*

I crawl up her belly, I kiss her lips, her closed lids. I return the favor of that forehead kiss.

Atop her, I reach over and pick up the phone. I dial next door.

I say, "Hey, Jimmy Lee. Can you come next door for a sec? Something you need to know, brother."

I let him in and we have it out. I'm left bloodied, a pulp. Delia leaves cloaked in tears, innocence, and Jimmy Lee, as I knew she would somehow.

> *"I don't melt*
> *when you walk in the room"*

9

I awake to another day. A voice on the television says it's August 16, anniversary of the death of the King, Babe Ruth, and Robert Johnson. My own birthday, too. I trudge to the bathroom for a look in the mirror, at my bloated face and busted lip.

I take a happy birthday piss. I take a happy birthday shower. I dry off. I get dressed. I go to the desk, find a piece of paper, write a note to Jimmy Lee. I write that I am sorry, that I am ashamed, weak, that I failed him, failed us all. I write, "A rock 'n' roll band may not seem like much to fail at, but it's what I've got. It's what I had. We all did."

I take the other paper, the paper with the song on it, and write atop it, below the title, "Words and music by James Lee Vine."

I find an envelope in the drawer and stuff the note and the song inside it. I seal the envelope. I dress and leave the hotel in search of a stamp, a mailbox, strong drink.

I walk the city streets and end up at the river, as if by summons. The river seems neither to notice nor care.

PART V

Ghosts

1

The songs come in dreams: old string-band ballads, backwoods rants, and other cries for help. The songs play in my head as gray, grainy images of hills pass into one another like folds of a blanket. In the dreams, my playing is precise, my singing sure. I don't need a band. The pretty girls ask what I drive and I say, "A '53 Wurlitzer. You oughta see it go."

I'm roused by the rain and the breeze it's brought along. I sit on the edge of the bed in the dark. Hands fumble for the guitar, head for the song. I strum in the dark. *The dark is my cowriter, there is nothing I shall want.*

I strum alone and imagine the rest—a blues harp so low, barely a sound at all, like sighs of the left-behind, then building slowly, like a faraway train or an advancing army. And over the hill it comes, around the bend with a faint light leading. The harp squawks and the harp honks. The harp sounds like many harps, a flock. Drums thump. A lead guitar plays a hook you can hang from, swing from. So maybe I want a band, need a band, after all.

Want and need—cowriters of all the best songs.

The darkness lies heavy like a comforting quilt; in the dark, I can find my way. The songs sometimes vanish in the light, nocturnal creatures with lost nerve. I wonder if that's the secret of the old blind blues singers, of Blind Lemon and Blind Blake, the Blind Willies, McTell and Johnson. Maybe I'll trick the light when it comes, close my eyes and clench them shut. I'll make art, or run into walls.

The rain picks up and the breeze kicks up. I wake up.

It's one o'clock in the morning and I'm parched.

I find the bed, the table beside the bed, turn on the light on the table beside the bed. I look about the room, a slow scan, as if checking for storm damage, looking for lost thoughts, fragments, shards of song.

I try to remember the song—to find it, retrieve it, repair it, nurse it to a hale and hearty state, hammer it into my memory and hang it from a hard-driven nail. *There, you fucker, you—got you.*

But it almost never happens. The songs scatter and stray—little prison breaks, they are. They flee to the corners and the ceiling, hide and huddle in the shadows, ride the fan blades and look down upon the utter folly of a man trying to nail a clump of dirt to the wall.

I almost forgot. I'm parched.

The day after the night before: I walk and wander. I work the alleys. Dark as tunnels, they are.

I find a bar and walk in.

It's called Two Steps From The Blues, after the Bobby "Blue" Bland classic. Beautifully sad and profound, that one. Oh, man, Bobby Bland. I imagine him as a weatherman for the worst of times, singing the five-day forecast: thunder, lightning, flash floods, biblical rains, and hell to pay. I order a beer from a woman the shade of the amber bottle she hands me.

I'm her only customer. I say hello after the fact, then ask her whose idea it was to put a bar in an alley.

"My uncle," she says with a smile about half-mean. "Brother of my dead daddy. I'm just helping him out *temporarily*." That last word bristles, ticks. And then, "The most famous barbecue restaurant in Memphis, it's in an alley."

"So he thought they were on to something, your uncle did?"

"Something like that," she says, and turns away, walks from behind the bar. She is tallish and thin with long black braids of hair, wears loose blue jeans, a gray T-shirt with the sleeves rolled up, feet bare.

I sip my beer. I ask if I can use the phone to call a cab. She says she'll call.

"Tell them to send somebody who knows where the bodies are buried," I say.

I don't quite hear what she tells the dispatcher—"Another live one," I think—but she lays down the receiver, turns to face me, and says it'll be a half-hour or so. She says Memphis is not a good town for cabs and so do I want another beer. I say that would be nice and ask for change for the jukebox.

The bar is one narrow room with black-and-white checker-board tiles, but the tiles are faded and cracked and the colors are dulling, the black meeting the white at a dingy gray. The gray stone walls are covered with framed album covers—B. B. King's live record from Ole Miss, an old Albert King from his Stax days, a Cannon's Jug Stompers collection—and spent instruments— mangled horns and busted guitars. The clock has stopped—no, there it is, the second hand lagging between ticks, slipping a little farther behind even as it moves forward.

I play Rufus Thomas's "Memphis Train," a huffing marvel of

hurtling soul, maybe the best train song ever. I wonder what it is about trains. Is it that they're a way out? Are they the means or the end?

I want to ask her what she thinks—I want to ask her thoughts on redemption, deceit, treachery, and momentum; I want to ask her about the inevitable fallibility of the male of the species; I want to ask her name—but I sit silently and drink, answer the cabbie's horn when it blows, and fairly skulk out of the place.

I have the cabbie drop me at the Graceland gates, as if I'm, you know, expected.

The tours have ended for the day. I walk up and down the sidewalk, reading the stone wall. Nearly every inch has been covered in prayers and scrawls, odes to Elvis and God, lightning bolts, song titles, snatches of movie dialogue. There's a slur against Colonel Parker and I wonder was that my daddy's. I'd shoved him from my mind since we hit town, but now, standing at the walls outside Graceland in the slumping light of day, I feel like John Gaunt's standing over my shoulder. I turn to see, but nothing—my own shadow, an emptying sidewalk, the slow crawl of traffic out on Elvis Presley Boulevard.

I turn back to the wall. Someone has drawn a crude cross on which a stick Elvis hangs. Below it is written,

> *sun & moon*
> *sin & moan*
> *how does it feel*
> *to be back home?*

I find a black pen on the sidewalk. I walk up and down, looking for a space to write. I find one finally, about the size and shape of a 45 rpm record's hole. It's a peephole into the past. It's history's perked ear, its pursed lips. There's no ink in the pen, so I use the point to carve into the wall. But the wall's too tough, the point breaks, and so much for that. I'm now officially pointless.

The cab is still sitting where it dropped me. I say to the driver, "Hollywood Cemetery."

Furry Lewis, the great bluesman and street sweeper, is buried there. It's not far. It's off the main drag, down a long, narrow road, then another. You pass another cemetery on the way to Hollywood. The one you pass is sprawling and green, the dead laid out gently under broad shade trees, wearing bright flowers as if on their lapels.

The cab rumbles on, pavement giving way to gravel. There's no gate, no stately entrance, nothing, just a black, busted mailbox sitting uneasily on a white wooden frame. I smile: a cemetery with a mailbox. *Furry, are you getting any mail these days?*

I ask the cabbie to wait, and start to wander. There's not much left of daylight, but the heat's hanging in. It's sticky, steamy, stuffy; it's hell, only hotter. The sun is a puffed-out chest. I follow the gravel road straight back into the cemetery, checking names as I go.

It's not hard to find. Furry's grave has two markers. One is small, rectangular, flush with the ground, gives his name, the dates of his birth and death, his occupation. No, not street sweeper for the City of Memphis Sanitation Department. Not that, but this:

Blues man

Behind the small marker is a three-foot-high monument, an acoustic guitar carved into granite. I heard money was taken up in Memphis bars to pay for this one and it's beautiful, it's grand in its near-about elegance.

I sit cross-legged on the ground before the grave. The ground has been baked, it's hard as concrete, keeps a good man down. Off in the near distance, I can see the other cemetery we passed. It's lush and comforting, this one stark as the truth. It says to the permanent guest and the casual visitor, *Nobody said death would be easy.*

The ground is cracked and I imagine Furry's blues breathing through. I imagine the sound of his guitar, the notes skipping, loping. I hear the voice of Furry as a young man: true and pure, detached somehow, as if he, Furry, were acting independent of good and evil, as if he had found a way to look down on both, the bemused observer. Which made him who, God?

Furry sang about guns, he sang about cemeteries, he sang about Memphis, Jackson, Chicago, and he sang about Cuba. He sang about mistreating mamas and mean old bedbugs, trains and train wrecks.

I pull a half-pint bottle of whiskey from my shirt pocket. I give Furry Lewis a splash and then take one for myself. I hit us again.

The cabbie's tapping his fingers, keeping time with the meter. I wave that I'll be a minute.

I'm half an hour and by the end of it I'm talking to Furry Lewis, one-legged wise-ass bluesman and street sweeper. But that's nothing. Furry's talking to me, too.

I ask for wisdom, truth, secret chords. I ask was Furry a fuck-up, too, and were his fuckups forgiven because of his agreeable nature and the wry little truths he sang to the world. I ask was he a loner, and a loner by choice, but did the women love him a world-record amount like I suppose they did.

" 'Nother splash of whiskey and I tell all," Furry says.

A splash for Furry, a drink for me, and the old man says, "Dead's better, most ways. Ain't got to get up, go to work. Ain't got to push that broom. Got people throwing money in a tin can with my picture on it. *My picture.* Handsome man, I am, but thirsty . . ."

Another splash.

"Got people come to see me. Was a blues band from Prague here t'other day. Prague. That shit ain't in Mi'sippi, son. A legend, I am, little bit of a tourist attraction. Thinking of pursuing the . . . what they say these days? Commercial potential. Build this place up. Tours and velvet ropes. Gift shop. Like Graceland, you know. Like Elvis's place. Good boy, Elvis. Good heart and a deep soul, raised right, had a good mama. But I was talking about me. Me and my place. Call it . . . Furryland."

I smile. I stand. I drain the bottle on the parched ground. The whiskey splashes up onto the monument, slides down its side, seeps into the ground.

I start to walk away. But Furry says, "I miss the pretty women. I miss the applause. I miss the lights. I miss those people I had at my feet the day I opened for the Rolling Stones over to Liberty Bowl Stadium. I miss sitting on my porch in the evening with my guitar on my lap, a jar close by. I even miss the hangovers. Nothing like the clanging of church bells to let you know you alive. Did I mention I miss the pretty women, son? I miss the ugly ones more. I miss walking the streets of Memphis with my one good leg."

I take one last look at the grave marker flush with the ground, then at the grand monument:

> *Walter "Furry" Lewis*
> *March 6, 1893*
> *Sept. 14, 1981*
>
> *When I lay my*
> *burden down*

I walk to the cab.

I sleep two days through and awake so groggy I think death has come and roughed me up. I shower and dress, begin to feel a little alive. I bound down the steps of the boardinghouse I now call home. Jimmy Lee's still at the hotel and Delia's there with him, I guess. Buck's disappeared.

I ran into him one night, down by the river. We didn't talk about Jimmy Lee and Delia. Not much, we didn't. Buck said he quit the band. I said I was surprised there was a band left to quit. Buck said he didn't need that noise. I said it was all my fault, said I was a sorry bastard.

"But mostly," I said, "I'm just sorry."

Buck said, *Yeah, yeah, but it was Delia. We should never have gotten tangled up with her.*

That's what Buck said, in so many words. Not many words. Mostly, I just read his nods.

One last nod said, *I couldn't have resisted her either. Wish she gave me a shot.* There was a faint smile that came with the nod.

I stood to go. I smiled faintly, too. "Down the road?" I said.

Sure, maybe.

So now I trudge the streets, feet dragging. I leave the streets for the alley, the alley for an alley bar.

2

"Some town you've got here," I say. "Ghosts all around."

Ida Queen is sitting on a barstool, down three from me. I'm facing the bar and she the barroom. She's told me her name. I've told her mine. She's barefoot in shorts; her brown legs aren't endless, but they go a good ways.

She turns and shakes her head, those long black braids of hair.

"*Ghosts,*" she says in a disgusted tone that would chase a few away. "That's the problem with this town. Stuck in the sad past. Won't get a move on."

"Forget about history, then?" I say. "Raze Sun Records like they razed Stax? Stop paying homage to Elvis and Furry and Otis and all the rest? Get on with things?"

"You're not as thick as I thought, white boy," she says, and flashes a smile with a knife edge to it.

I ask her to go out on the town with me. "We'll raze the place," I say. "Leave no building standing."

"No thanks. No, but thanks."

"Standing offer."

"It'll get tired of standing, after a spell."

She goes to sweep the bar and I go to the jukebox, to play her a blues.

Closing time. I help her shut down. She padlocks the door. She puts her hand on my shoulder, says, "You're seriously on the rebound, huh?"

"More like a ricochet. But yeah."

"Good night, anyway."

Ten feet away, she stops, turns, shakes her head, and goes on.

"Offer still stands," I say.

"It's already starting to slouch," she says. "Buck up, Luther Gaunt."

I stand in the dark and think of rebounds and ricochets and something that rhymes with bucking up. I think of what I'm doing, what I've done. I think of the band. I think of having lived life as if everything were a metaphor, a symbol for something else, until my life became flesh for those few moments with Delia. I see myself scurrying back now to the land of metaphor and symbolism. It's where I live and the mail is starting to pile up. The weeds are knee-high.

And I think about the old Cassandra Special Rider guitar, gone now. Think, *Am I truly cursed now or am I free of her finally? Am I free of them all? Am I a Gaunt in name only? Am I a blank white page? Can I write my own song now, my own ending?*

Another day. The days have become one.

"Some town," I say as we sit on the front stoop of the bar. In my mind, I can see through the alley, around the bends and corners, can see the big river flowing. I see ghosts gone back to flesh. I hear music playing, see a dance floor filling up, feel her thin, dark body on my pale, gaunt one.

Ida Queen says, "Memphis is a funeral home with a gift shop."

We take a drive in the Merc. We pick up a six-pack of beer. We park on the bluff overlooking the river.

"Elvis used to bring his best girl here," I say. "Imagine that. I'm sitting where Elvis sat and you're sitting where Elvis's best girl sat."

I smile and amend that: "Well, Elvis's best girl might have been over here, too, crawling into the pocket of Elvis's Crown Electric work shirt."

I pop the tops on a couple of beers. I light a cigarette.

It's going for dark, but still it's stifling out. The only air is the river's breath, a sweet, warm stench that climbs the bluff in a slow rush.

"I can see him now," Ida says. "Elvis just a-sitting there, taking it easy after a long day of stealing the black man's music."

"You don't believe that, do you?"

She shifts toward the river, her dark, small back to me. She looks over her shoulder. "I don't know, Luther Gaunt. I don't guess." She turns back toward the window, the river.

"Elvis said, 'I don't sound like nobody.' And he didn't. Didn't look like nobody either."

"You sweet on him or something, white boy?"

"I'm just saying."

I put in a CD of Elvis's comeback record. Elvis is singing "I'm Movin' On," the old Hank Snow number. It starts as a country trot, then comes to the big city, becomes a soul strut. I drink to

Elvis and his pretty mama. I drink to the moment. I look at Ida Queen and the great river beyond and I believe in . . . oh, what the hell, possibilities.

"Where I come from, we had just a little river. Nothing really special," I say. "Not the Mississippi, but then what is?"

"The Nile," she says.

"You really don't think this place is anything so special?"

"I guess it once was. Before my time. Now it's neither here nor there. I'm thinking of maybe going to Atlanta. Moving there."

"Well, Ida Queen, Queen Ida, I'll tell you what. I believe in Memphis, the great lost city of sound. I believe it'll come back. I believe there are untold hit songs waiting to be written and sung. I believe the world's leaning toward Memphis, whether it realizes it or not, craning to hear. I believe in the second coming of Otis—maybe he's white this time, and has a fear of flying—and of Elvis—maybe he's black and will refuse to become some ol' carny's movie prop. I believe this city is sad and blue and rather tired at the moment, but there's all manner of crazy shit bubbling under. There always is. The river brings a new supply every day. I believe Sam Phillips may be long done cutting records, but he left a map, or crumbs, or something, to follow. I believe Johnny Cash has another decade of songs in him. I believe crazy-ass Rufus Thomas will live forever. And I believe Jerry Lee Lewis has one more comeback in him, and this time it won't matter if he marries a farm animal."

Ida shakes her head, says, "That so, white boy?"

I shrug.

We drain our beers and I drive Ida Queen home.

Another day. I sit on one barstool, prop my feet on another, guitar in hand. It's the first one I've played since I busted Cassie to splinters. Ida found it in a back room. I pick at the strings. I search for words and watch her move, a bold italic letter struck upon on a blank white page.

"I'm going to do what Elvis did," I say.

Ida Queen stops. She leans the broom against the gray stone wall. "Fake your death?"

I watch her watching me watching her: Ida Queen, Queen Ida. I'm going to ask her to marry me. I haven't done that in about three beers. My blues song isn't happening. Nothing is. Fame isn't. Not that fame is what we Long Gone Daddies were ever about, what I ever craved. But I suppose it was, in its way. Fame on my terms.

> *I'm a 45 rpm*
> *I'm two minutes, ten*
> *I'm the sound*
> *you can't get out*
> *of your head*

Famous Luther Gaunt.

Fame us, Luther Gaunt.

I'm not even sure obscurity is within reach now. Obscurity suggests somebody out there knows you exist—some skinny teenage boy in a small, gray Northern city, with his stereo and his angst. Rock wouldn't roll without skinny teenage boys, their stereos, and their angst.

> *I'm hard-pressed on vinyl*
> *Who'll rock you like I will?*

Delia was right. When you play in a band, you have delusions of double platinum.

I can play it fast
I can go way slower
My highs are high
my lows are even lower

Luther Gaunt: plays scruffy little songs on an old guitar. Leaps about, flails and wails. Please the fans, Luther: fan them. Leave no rock unrolled, no riff unraffed. Leave them spent and sated and back to the suburbs they go. The *sub urbs*, like some place you burrow to.

Luther Gaunt on stage, flinging himself in a most frightful way, as if drugs and lightning hit him at the same time, threw dice for possession. Then standing still, a statue of one more singer who thinks he has something to say—one more singer who swears he won't sell out, and wonders who'd buy it if he did.

So if you don't like this side of me
flip me over

There's not much in the way of air conditioning in the bar. A couple of window units labor against the heat, groaning and wheezing; it sounds like there's about to be an explosion down at the accordion factory.

I sit on the barstool, play at playing this new old guitar, and watch Ida sweep the floor.

"Let me get that."

"Nah, I got it."

"C'mon."

"Nah, you play."

Ida Queen, black girl who doesn't like the blues. Queen Ida, whose history she'd just as soon sweep into a dustpan.

"Bukka White," I say, because maybe saying the name will

summon the spirit and sway this strayed soul.

"Who's Bukka White?"

"Oh, Bukka, man. He was raw. He was real. Bukka sang the blues. Bukka did time. Bukka hated that name. Booker T. Washington White was his proper name."

"You want to know what I think of that?" Ida Queen says. "The one you call Bukka ought not have done what he did to do time. That'll get you called a lot of things you don't like."

"He lived in Memphis," I say. "There was this one day, rain pouring. This was after he did what he ought not to have done to do the time, after he'd done that time. He opened the door and there stood his cousin or nephew, one. I can't remember which. Anyway, his name was Riley B. King, up from Itta Bena or Indianola, thereabouts. It was Riley B. King, young and thin, standing at the door in the rain, wearing the storm. I'm not making this up. It happened. Something like it. I may have added the rain for dramatic effect. This was here. This was your town, Memphis."

"Not my town," Ida says, unmoved. "Got enough to do to sweep this bar."

I sit on the barstool, sip my beer.

"Do you believe in the redemptive power of the river, Ida Queen?"

It's only us in the bar. Nobody comes here.

"I believe the river takes what the river wants," Ida says over her shoulder.

"What about those people Tom Lee saved from drowning, all those many years ago? They named the park down by the river for him. They put up a marker."

"I said the river takes what the river *wants*." She leans on the word.

"Yeah, well."

I sit and wonder what to believe in. I decide to go on believing in the redemptive power of the river. I decide to take another drink. What else?

Unsmash my guitar.

Fake my death.

Write a blues song.

Ida Queen, Queen Ida, is walking away now, walking away before I can finish the story, before the part about how Bukka White's thin rail of a rain-drenched cousin or nephew, I can't remember which, became B. B. King and the world changed its tune. He changed it, with that sweet sting of strings and that high, church wail.

"Marry me, Ida Queen!" I shout across the room, across black-and-white checkerboard tiles swept clean.

Ida's leaning against the back-door frame, bright sun on brown skin sweating. Ida's eyes roll behind long black braids of hair.

"You going to want to fake your marriage, too?"

3

Elvis levitates as the children climb the metal sculptures surrounding him, paying him no royal mind. Dusk on the river bluff, a jug band playing in the gazebo as dancers dance on scuffed concrete. Mosquitoes hovering. Sensing him sucked dry, the dancers pay Elvis no mind either.

Consider: Elvis as bronze statue—young, lean, mythic, with a fringed jacket and guitar flashing, a curled lip you could smash bottles against—levitating with the aid of black iron bars and stout yellow straps. The Elvis statue is in for repairs at the National Ornamental Metal Museum, up high on the bluff, looking down.

Consider: the King, weather-beaten and time-ravaged, carved into and written on, "FOREVER ELVIS" scrawled in black letters across his crotch.

I lie some twenty yards away, on my side, facing the river, eyes on its curves. I look up into an orange and peach sky through tall, bushy trees, watch it turn purple, then blue, dark, then darker, then disappearing.

"You have the best sunsets here," I say.

"That's because we don't have mountains," Ida says. "Other places, they have mountains. Mountains would be nice."

"Mountains just block the view."

"Mountains *are* the view, white boy."

She smiles through a frown. She hands me a plastic cup.

"Memphis Mai Tai," she says. "Beer and bug spray."

We drink our drinks. Ida asks what happened to the band and I tell her all about it.

"Long Gone Daddies, like some damn old country song?"

"It was," I say. "Hank Williams."

"Why didn't you name yourselves after a Memphis bluesman, not some country hick from wherever?"

"Alabama. Where Hank Williams was from."

"Alabama," she says, as if it were off somewhere in the Third World, instead of standing between her and Atlanta.

"Well, I sort of come from a long line of gone daddies. My daddy, and his, too. It's not a pride thing, especially. More like full disclosure. So I couldn't resist. That, and it's not such a stretch from country to the blues, really. Hank played the blues. His first music lessons came from this black guy named Tee-Tot. Anyway, it's all one South, one mixed-up stew of sound. And if you want to dig deeper for meaning in it, you could say that Memphis—Elvis, rock 'n' roll, all that—is what would have killed Hank Williams if pain and pills and hooch hadn't gotten him first."

"Memphis just the death of everybody, huh, white boy?"

"I don't know. We're still kicking."

Ida stands and walks to the dance floor and I follow. I don't know how to dance to jug band blues, the way they scoot on by, way they chug. I dance like a man out on a ledge. The street had better watch out below; I'm a lot of dead weight these days.

Ida flows, loose and liquid: the river embodied. I want to hold her, hang on and become her. I want to climb her, kiss her, right here with the mosquitoes buzzing, the dancers dancing, dead Elvis levitating, as Furry Lewis sings about those Memphis women.

The song ends and I say, "That was a Furry Lewis number. That there."

"Sorry name for a man," she says. "I guess that's better than Tee-Tot. But still. *Furry*."

"Well, Walter was his given name."

"That's better. Proper. What the hell kind of job's a man going to get calling himself Furry?"

"Furry was a street sweeper."

"Well, that's one."

"And he sang the blues, you know. He opened for the Rolling Stones one time at Liberty Bowl Stadium."

"You mean he swept the stage for them?"

"Jesus, you're a case, Ida Queen."

She turns her face away, but there's a smile on it.

I give her room as she dances. I move enough to make like I'm dancing, but mostly I'm watching her, watching from the concrete dance floor to the depths of the deep, dark blue-black sky. I settle on her eyes. Shade of midnight: the blues embodied.

I move closer now to her, and she moves into me, and her lips to my ear, and certain words are whispered.

Says Ida Queen, black girl who doesn't like the blues, to pale, white Luther Gaunt, lost soul of rock 'n' roll, "You want to fuck a black woman or be a black man? Which is it, white boy?"

We take a break from dancing. We're eating pork shoulder and drinking beers.

"So you don't want to marry me," I say.

"I don't want to *anything* you," she says, then smiles faintly, a splash of pity in it. "No offense."

"But you're here with me, Ida Queen."

"You're a pest," she says. "You're a mosquito. I wave you away and here you are. You've got it hard. Look at you. Poor, pale Luther Gaunt. Can't change his skin, but that won't stop him from trying. Finds himself a brown-skin girl, hovers and buzzes. Whether he's after the brown-skin girl or the blues itself—a song, *the* song—is another matter. Brown-skin girl, by the way, doesn't like the blues. Imagine that. Never heard of Bukka White, who ought not have done what he did to do time, but did it, and so he had to do it. Time, I mean. And rail-thin Riley B. King, without the sense to come in out of the rain. Never paid any of them any mind. Prefers her music to be slick and smooth. Uptown. Doesn't want to be reminded of the old days. Field hands, all of them. Doesn't want to know. Brown-skin girl happens to sweep a floor but doesn't intend to make a career of it. College girl with dreams—no, in*ten*tions—of becoming a professional. Business. You've heard of business, haven't you, Luther? Have a place of my own and damn sure not in an alley. Single-minded, this girl. No time for the old songs. She's not inclined. *Ain't* going back. Hmm. But does seem to be dancing to these blues. She'll give them that."

She turns and walks away, toward the river.

"That's something," I say.

I watch Ida doze on the riverbank, brown skin on dirt like her roots are there. My pale hand hovers and buzzes. *Mosquito: blood sucker.*

Ida: slight girl, all eyes, opens and closes them, shuttered windows to truth, wonder, suspicion, doubt, blues songs. The slats open. I steal a glance.

I'm sitting on the riverbank watching her seep into the ground. I'm losing her.

You can't lose what you never had.

The hell you can't.

I want to go away, forever far, Ida in gentle tow. I want to try for some distant shore, and once there sort the real from the imagined, metaphor from flesh, and from what's left fashion a way of living, a life.

I crouch by the river watching, listening. I wake Ida. We walk to the car. She's wobbly; she's woozy. I'm a wall she leans on. It's midnight now; many hours and much alcohol have passed—lot of kick in the bug spray tonight. The resolve's leaving her now. Resolve falling down like rain. Coming a storm.

I drive her home. I carry her upstairs, lay her in her bed. I run a pale hand through long black braids of hair. A peck on Ida Queen's cheek and a finger to Queen Ida's lips as she stirs: *Shh.*

I leave her apartment and walk the city.

Memphis, Tennessee.

Home of the Blues.

Birthplace of Rock 'n' Roll.

Soulsville USA.

I bump into B. B. dripping wet and wailing, Jerry Lee joyriding over slick streets, Rufus T. in satin shorts, singing "Walking the Dog." Otis is soul-shouting about sweet music. Furry's giving guitar lessons to Elvis, the boy King, saying, *You'll get it yet and wish you hadn't, E: the blues.*

The day's drawing nigh, pulling up in a white stretch limo, like a hearse with a wet bar. As if to say, *Will you be in it, Luther Gaunt? We need a body for a funeral.*

I wander into a bar. A song gives the time of day: "Three O'Clock Blues." A man pushes a broom and nods. Pale hand around the scruff of a longneck. Stray shots. Pack of smokes. Quarter still buys three tunes on the '53 Wurlitzer.

I walk the streets and my footsteps are her heartbeat. The river breeze is the brush of her eyelashes. The traffic lights are her bold, blinking eyes.

I'll forget her in time. Thousand years or so.

Luther's blue. Luther's blues.

Sing them, Luther.

PART VI

Fathers and Sons

1

Early Sunday morning. South Main in Memphis.

I'm down on all fours, sick as the whipped dog I've become. I retch onto the weeds and sidewalk cracks outside Central Station. I retch some more—the rotgut of my follies, the Robert Johnson death-scene reenactment blues, every last drop of last night's drink. I shudder, I shake. I lower my head about to the pavement. I retch yet again. No, not my finest moment, good people, but I've never felt more a Gaunt.

I push myself up. I stand, but just barely—a stoop borrowed from some old man who wasn't using it anymore. I take two halting steps and then halt. Down on all fours again, I retch.

I fall onto my side, try to fight the tug of sleep. I breathe deep my own stench and that does it. My eyes pop open. The sun plays hell on my pounding head. I push myself off the sidewalk, onto my knees now.

I see I have company. I'm thinking Memphis's finest.

But no.

The car is long and powder blue. It eases to a stop beside me and the driver says over the hum of the idling engine, "My, but aren't you a ball off the ol' chain."

And now he's out of the car and standing over me, a hand on my shoulder, saying, "Let's get you cleaned up, son. Let's get you showered and rested and then see what we got."

My daddy pours me into the backseat of that car all powder blue and endless and I'm asleep upon impact with the white leather seats.

I awake to the smell of black coffee on the bedstand, soul oldies on the radio. I sit on the edge of the bed, sip the coffee. My head's only pounding now. I stand and start to wander. It's a small, old house with plank-wood floors. In the bathroom, I take a piss and a good, long look at myself in the mirror. I could use a shave and some shearing to my hair, but otherwise I don't look too awfully bad for a man descended so recently from dog.

I leave the bathroom for a hallway, the white walls bare of pictures. I leave the hall for a mostly bare living room. There's an old couch, a chair, an upturned crate for a table. I recognize the decorating style—Early Itinerant Musician. I walk outside to the front porch. There sits my daddy in a metal folding chair, reading the morning newspaper.

"One time, I slept two days through," he says. "Never done three."

"I miss anything?"

"Stuff and things, you know. But not really, no. There's a little

bit about your gal Delia in the paper. She's getting herself a big
Nashville recording contract, looks like."

"Well, that's a shocker—Delia getting what she wants. Anyway, that's what I was trying to sleep off. You know, stuff and
things."

"Yeah, well. I've been there, Luther. I've been there with bells
on."

I sit on the porch railing, back against a pillar. I look out onto
the leafy street, at my daddy's powder-blue car. It seems to be a
Caddy. It's a big, long stretch of ride and I wonder about my own
muddy-brown Merc. I seem to have misplaced it.

"Well, I hated for you to see me like that, Daddy."

"It was good just to see you at all, son."

"How'd you know I'd be there?"

John Gaunt sets the newspaper on the porch beside him,
shifts his weight on the metal folding chair. He's looking out
upon that leafy street, too, at the powder-blue car. I guess we
haven't gotten to that point where we can just look each other
square in the eye.

"Well, I didn't, exactly. But let's just say you've been traveling
a small world these last few weeks. Anyway, I've been watching
you almost since you hit Memphis. Doc Wise, he's a friend. We
go back a ways. So I was there those nights when you and the
band were tearing up the Furry Dice and I was there those nights
when your gal Delia started to sing that song."

"One Night of Sin."

"That one, yep. Well, and I was there those nights when it
became her stage and her band for no other reason than that's
what she wanted. Some folks, son, they think life's a pizza you
order. And for some folks, it is."

"You were there." I almost look him in the eye.

"Way in the back. And yeah, I was there when the place was near empty with you alone up on that stage. I heard you play those sad ones and heard you come out of it, play those mean ones. I saw you bust up that old guitar. Not thinking that the best time to reveal myself, I slid out the door then."

"I'm sorry."

"About the guitar?"

"It was yours. It was your daddy's. Cassandra. Cassie. Cass."

"Yeah, well. It's no big thing, Luther." He pauses and grins. I can see the grin from the corner of my eye. "Not anymore, it ain't."

"But it's what ties us all together. It's the symbol for all we've ever been. The Gaunt line."

"Well, then, busted is about right, I'd say. Should've been done years ago. Wish I'd thought of it."

I turn to look at him. He's long, tall, and lanky, in that Gaunt way. He has a full head of gray-streaked black hair. His face is heavily lined, but he's clean-shaven and his eyes call to mind hubcaps with still some shine under all that road dust. I always thought he'd look like death's crazy uncle by the time I found him, if I found him—not that I was particularly looking.

He seems to be looking at me as if he knows what I'm thinking. He smiles.

"Anyway, there are other trees and other guitars," he says. "You ought to get you one of those that plug in. A shiny, black one, say, with a big amp about yea high." He pushes out of that folding chair, unfolds himself from it.

I meet him at the top step. "You think so?"

"Yeah. You know what they say?"

"What's that, Daddy?"

"Every generation discovers electricity for itself."

2

We take a drive in the big powder-blue car. It moves like a good run of days.

We drive the streets of the city, the radio tuned to the soul oldies station.

"Memphis," my daddy says. "Damnedest place ever was, but I do love it. Memphis slouches and Memphis grins and Memphis is real, in the best and worst ways and most ways in between."

"Memphis, with its chin stubble," I say. "Memphis, with a song lounging there with an unlit cigarette on those licked lips."

"Rock 'n' roll, yeah," my daddy says. "Three chords, piss, and hokum. You hear what I'm saying, son?"

"I hear you, Daddy. I hear you."

We stop for barbecue at a converted gas station not far from downtown.

Standing at the register, waiting, he says, "And how's your mother?"

"She's fine."

"Okay, then."

We pick up a twelve-pack of beer at a convenience store on the drive home. We drink the beer and eat that barbecue on the porch of the little house on the leafy street.

"Well, I think about her," he says.

"I know you do."

"I know that's not the same thing as doing anything about it."

"No, but maybe it's a start."

"Well," he says.

We pop the tops on fresh beers. We clink cans.

"To rock 'n' roll," he says.

"Three chords, piss, and hokum."

"To Memphis."

"Sure, what the hell. To Memphis."

We have a good run of days.

We sit on the front porch in the mornings, drinking coffee and reading the newspaper. One day, there's a story about plans to build a museum to Stax Records. My daddy says they're talking about putting it down on Beale Street. He says they ought to just put the damn thing on that empty lot where Stax Records used to be. "Full circle," he says, "like some old record spinning round, you know, son?"

I say I know. And I tell him about Ida Queen, what she said about Memphis being a funeral home with a gift shop.

"Yeah, well," my daddy says. "There is that. But the old songs still sound sweet. The young ones can't help but hear them, even if they don't realize. They may carry it on, in their way. Make those old songs their own. Make them new."

He eases out of his chair, stretches and yawns and says, "Barbecue run?"

Most afternoons, we go for long drives in the powder-blue Caddy. We keep the windows down and turn the music up loud. The wind whips and there's not much talking to be done.

This one day, we drive down south of Memphis, into Mississippi. Off in the distance, kudzu has grown to the size of mountains, taken on the form of beasts. The beasts dance a stomp on the flatland. "The Kudzu Ruins of Upper Mississippi," my daddy, John Gaunt, says, and sings,

> *I'm a kudzu vine*
> *I'm a kudzu vine*
> *That's what I wanna be*
> *I wanna crawl and creep*
> *I wanna spread my leaf*
> *I wanna cover you with me*

His voice shares some qualities with the hum of the engine. It's not a pretty voice, but it can take you places you might not otherwise have ventured. It's a fearless, knowing voice. My daddy sings the words again and lets them drift away as we leave Highway 61 for some little country lane. My daddy drives slowly now, at barely more than a poke.

"In fact," he says, picking up the loose thread of a conversation we've had only in his head, "I've been home a few times to see her. But see her is all I did. I watched her while she sat on the back porch, reading on those books of hers. I watched her run errands downtown. She's a fine-looking woman, still. She's a fine-looking woman with sad eyes. One day, I watched her stand on the top step out in front of the house as the sun went down, her just standing there and thinking . . . what? One night, she had the windows open and the shades were up, and she put on that one record of mine and she danced all alone to it. I just about up and walked through the front door. But I thought better. Or anyway, I thought different."

We come to a little crossroads. There's a hand-painted sign, white with black lettering, that says, *Jesus is coming are you ready?* Beyond that, after a left turn, another sign says, *Well?*

My daddy smiles and says, "I don't know what it says about me, but I've always found Mississippi a more fascinating place than outer space. Not that I've been to outer space, mind you. Just going by what I hear." He has an easy smile. He always did, the son of a bitch.

Smooth road gives way to tamped gravel and dirt. Another sign says, in so many breathless words we have to stop to read them all, *Jesus was here where were you He waited and waited but you never came He left where were you probably off whore mongering up in sinful Memphis.*

"This is not really any of my business, but . . ."

"Shoot, Luth."

"Just how lousy of a spouse were you? I mean, beyond the fact that you rarely came home and then quit coming home altogether, how bad were you?"

John Gaunt eases his foot onto the accelerator but goes only a hundred yards before the road stops. The road is overgrown with scruff and junk—couch cushions, a child's bicycle, a car's front bumper, a barstool, TV, a kitchen sink. It's like one of those kudzu monsters has taken a house, broken it over its knee, and shaken out its contents here.

My daddy sighs. He looks out at that mess just ahead. There's not enough room to turn around, so he cuts the engine and says, "I didn't set up house with a woman not my pregnant wife and then proceed to get that woman pregnant, too. I never did that. I did other things, though."

"You don't have to tell me them. That's not what I'm asking."

"He was the granddaddy of all rounders, my old man. I've talked to enough people who knew him to know that. He was a great guitar player with those long fingers of his. His fingers went on forever, you know, like some women's legs and some country lanes. Not this one, though. This one's at the end of its line, it seems."

He sighs. He smiles at me. "And he had a smooth-talking way of singing, your granddaddy. Women loved him. He could have looked plug-ugly and still done just fine, with all those other things going for him. But he didn't. From the pictures and from what my own ma told me, he was big and a Gaunt version of strapping. But he wasn't a rough one. He was a pushover. Women liked that about him. He'd fall for them and them for him. Looking at it from some distance, you can judge the man—hell, he knocked up that Wanda while my mother, after a series of miscarriages over lots of years, was carrying me, so I can damn straight judge the man—but you can also see that he didn't have much cause to change. What I mean is, Luther, his weaknesses must've felt strangely like strengths to him. They got him drunk and they got him laid and, Lord, but did they ever get him some songs."

"Well," I say.

"And in the end, they got him shot, too. Like I used to tell you, remember? The morning of the day, like I used to say. The morning of the day your granddaddy Malcolm was to go and record for Mr. Sam Phillips, that musician named Frankie Walls came home to find Malcolm shacked up with Frankie's wife, in Frankie's house."

I tell him I know all that. I tell him I've heard the stories, read the newspaper clippings, pieced it together.

I say, "So Mr. Sam, he just had to make do with Elvis and Johnny and Carl and Jerry Lee and the rest." I manage a smile.

We sit there saying nothing and then he sings the one about kudzu again, the whole song this time.

"That's one by your granddaddy," he tells me. "I imagine he had a way of singing it that the ladies loved. They loved to get all tangled up in him, is my guess. Anyway, I found the lyrics, written by the man's own hand, in a box in the attic of my house. Well, not my house. I rent it by the month."

"That house? That's the house where . . . ?"

"Three eighty-two Patton. Everybody has to live somewhere."

"Did you . . . ?" I don't know what it is I want to ask, exactly.

"Did I just want to somehow be close to my long gone daddy?" He pushes open the car door, unfolds himself from behind the wheel. He stands and stretches and walks around to the hood. He takes a seat and I join him. "Yeah, I did. And is that pretty much the reason you came to Memphis?"

"That's part of it, yeah. That, and it's Memphis. You know? I wanted to chase and catch those ghosts and buy them beers and hear their stories. I wanted to see what the river had to say. I wanted to sink in the sacred muck, become something deeper than I was. I wanted, you know, to walk on whiskey. Rock 'n' roll. Like you say, three chords, piss, and hokum. You hear what I'm saying, Daddy?"

"I hear it, son. Been hearing it all my born days."

"And I thought I'd find you, see you, talk to you. I thought it might be in some gutter that I found you. I'm sorry, but it's true.

I figured the years had caught you and roughed you up. I'm sorry about this, too, but I think that's how I wanted to find you. I love you, but I wanted to see you low-down and suffering, because I love my ma—your wife—and she never gave me—never gave you—any cause to be anything less than devout at her feet. I keep saying it, but I'm sorry."

"Don't be sorry." He lies back on the hood. "All that happened. Too much of living in the small hours, too much drink. Oh, I was a sight. I looked like something Frankie Walls wouldn't've wasted a bullet on."

"So what happened?"

"Well, son, the bottom hurts when you hit it. It jars you. It did me. So I just sort of straightened up then. I quit playing music. I mailed you the old family guitar. I was drinking like they weren't making more, so I quit that. I take it slow now. I took regular work. I drove a cab and I tended bar. Lately, I've been helping this buddy of mine who has a little record label. He loves music without knowing much about it. He just knows that it's a beautiful thing. So it seems I'm the in-house producer. He seems to think the world's craving to hear what Memphis might sing next. He's got enough money to think what he wants. It's old Memphis money. He's a good guy, got a good heart. His ear is true, though I suspect he's coming close to losing about as much money as his cotton-king daddy will allow. Anyway, it's his car—one of his. He lets me drive it."

> *The car was powder-blue and endless*
> *like a good run of days*

I wish I had a guitar to pick up the trail, set it to music. An old Cassandra the color of whiskey and water would be nice— yeah, and with a gold ring of flowers around the sound hole, a gift to the sad songs of the dark hollow within. But anything with strings would do.

We go silent, the sky to gray. Dark comes and paves the sky black. We get in the car and he backs all the way down that dead end of a country lane, like playing a record backwards.

3

The next morning, I awake to an empty house. There's coffee in the kitchen, and a note. My daddy says he's gone to his buddy's recording studio. He gives the address and directions, says I should come by.

I sit on the kitchen counter, where I imagine my daddy's daddy sat strumming the old guitar and singing songs of Eula. I tell the ghosts to keep it down. I've got a phone call to make.

"Tell me a story, Ma."

"A story, Luther?"

"Your story, Ma. The one about you, starring you."

She doesn't say anything for the longest time, but it's a comfortable silence. It's like she's gathering memories to give me.

"I was born in the backseat of a cab in the alley," she begins. "Ours was a town of alleys. It's how you got from one place to the other—to the store, to school, and back home. It's how the men got from one bar to the next. Shortest distance between two pints, you could say."

She pauses, as if to let a ghost pass.

"From our little town, you could probably get to the city, Scranton, by taking nothing but alleys. Scranton was gray and shrinking. The coal industry was all but dead. But we got by. We didn't know any better. We didn't know New York City or Paris. We didn't have big, long boulevards"—she takes her time with that last word, as if she's walking the length of one slowly, savoring every step—"but, you know, I liked those alleys. I did. They were cramped and narrow and littered with all manner of things. Beer cans, cigarette wrappers, gnawed lollipop sticks, an empty pint of Old Somebody. You might see anything. Doll parts—an arm, a foot, a hank of hair. Bent and mangled coat hangers. A slingshot. A pocketknife. Weapons, you know. Trash-can lids were discarded shields. Where you look for drama, Luther, you find it. I'd see specks of blood—what I hoped, somehow, was blood. Tobacco spit, oil splotches. Our alleys shimmered with oil splotches. And there was pigeon shit, you know, and coal dust. And there was an old library chair somebody'd thrown out, wooden and wobbly, and a girl sitting in it, legs curled under her and a book in her small hands."

She pauses again, this time to gaze upon her own ghost.

"I always was reading. I read everything I could find. Dickens and Jane Austen and more Dickens. The Brontë sisters. The Beats. Science fiction. I'd sit outside in the alley in that library chair, a book in one hand and a cigarette in the other. I was fifteen and felt ancient, like I'd somehow outlived everybody and now it was just me with my books. I'd sit in the alley with an afghan around me until my fingers froze and couldn't turn another page, and then I'd go inside and find a floor to curl up on.

My mother cleaned the house around me, lifted my feet and ran the sweeper underneath, nudged my elbow to brush a dust rag across the baseboard. She didn't yell. A little, is all. I was her little scholar. My mother, who otherwise never spoke of sex in any regard, said I'd make a lousy prostitute because I'd just lie there—probably with a book still in my hand. She laughed when she said it, though. My older sister called me names, said books never put a meal on a table, stoked a fire, knitted an afghan to keep anyone warm when there was no fire left to stoke. In the winter, there was ice on the insides of the windows. The shapes, you know, were pretty. Hieroglyphics, cave art. I don't know. It's amazing what fascinates you."

She sighs and says, "Ours was not a house of readers. Though my father, who was a welder, he made up words. *Scuthy*. That was one of his. It was a word you could drop into most any sentence spoken in our town. Our town was called Foley. It had a lot of Irish in it. The next little town over was Amato, where the Italians lived. Nothing was sacred in Foley. All was scuthy. *Choaste* was another of my father's words. I don't know how to spell it or what it's a cross between, but you can tell what it means by hearing it. You got choasted from your job if you were nothing but a layabout, if you were dipping in the till. You got choasted from the bars if you got too rowdy. Not a lot did, though. The bars were sad, quiet places—thin, serious men hunched over short glasses of beer. There were lots of bars in Foley. There was the Happy Guest and Fahey's Famous. There was Burke's and Daly's Lament and Muldoon's. My father used to say he was going 'down the alley.' That's what he called it when he went to the bar. When I was a little girl, my father would bring me 45 rpm records. He knew the guy who stocked the jukeboxes. I remember getting those early Beatles songs. Those boys, they'd heard all those old songs out of Memphis and other places and they were singing them back to America, in their own way and their own voices. I didn't know that then. I knew it later. Your daddy told me. And there were other records. There were girl singers, too. I remember that one by the Ronettes, 'Be My Baby.' "

"That's a good one."

"I'd stand in front of the mirror, mimic them singing that song. I'd stand before the mirror, wishing for hips, for hairpin curves, a sexy voice." She sighs again, wistfully, as if she's tousling the hair of her own ghost. "Well, anyway, a man my father knew, a man he drank with, sold books. I don't know how he made a living at that, in these parts. But anyway, he did. He gave my father some books to give to me. My father brought home bound copies of Hemingway, Fitzgerald, Dos Passos. I tore through the pages like fire."

She steps out of the story, says it's starting to snow there. "It's way early this year and that's fine. I loved winter most of all," she says. "Snow fell thick and white, bunched at the edges of the streets and alleys like tucking the town in for the night. I slept well those nights. I fell deep and dreamed long and awoke to all possibilities. Every other day, you know, greeted you with a stare. But on those snowy days, you could go anywhere, do anything, be anybody. The English countryside of Austen could be under all that snow. Streets of Paris. Battlefields. Frozen oceans. Lost cities. I'd lie in the snow in the middle of the alley, my arms outstretched, then bring them in slowly."

"Angel wings."

"The hell!" my mother says with delight. "I wanted to be an anarchist, a gun moll, a rabble-rouser, things I'd read about in books. The world was in those books. The world was a big, unruly mess captured by some writer and set wild on the page. You know the best thing about a book, a really good one, Luther?"

"What's that, Ma?"

"The next page. The next thing that happens. The next person, next place. It keeps a person going."

"I can see that, Ma."

"And in my story, what happened next was I met a boy. I was sitting in the alley and he was running through it. He was running like he was being chased—like he wanted me to think he was being chased. I don't know what it was about him. I guess it was everything about him. He seemed like some boy out of a story. He didn't know what would happen next, but he knew something would. He ran through that alley the next day and the next, and then one day he came through the alley but not running. I guess you'd call him handsome. He was when he sang, I know that. He sang to me. He sang while I read and it was all I could do to keep the story straight. I don't know what he saw in me. There were prettier girls. But he didn't have to run and fake a chase to get them and I think he liked it, that he had to work a little, use his wiles, just to get me to look up and see something that wasn't stamped on a page. I wasn't playing hard to get, you know. What I mean is, I wasn't playing. I didn't want a boyfriend, but all of the sudden I had one. He had a band and they were already playing shows out of town. But turns out we were good at being apart together. That's what I called it. It's pretty much a necessity, Luther, if you want to marry a musician. So after we graduated high school, we got married and I got pregnant, and the next year I had you. It was the year of the flood. But Scranton didn't get hit so badly, not like Wilkes-Barre. I guess it would have made the story more dramatic if it did. You know how I love a dramatic story. Our alleys would have become canals and our cabs gondolas. But you weren't born in the alley, Luther. It was the hospital for you. It was you and me, son. God, the sight of you. The handsome little mug of a face."

"My daddy . . ."

"He wasn't there, no. He called, though. Well, he called back after he got the message."

"Well, you know," I say. "Musicians. They're not so good at changing."

She sighs. She says, "Well, I haven't changed all that much over the years either. I don't sit in a chair in the alley anymore, but I think about it when I stand at the window and look outside, like now. Snow's starting to pile up, Luther. You should see it."

"I think Memphis just sort of turns gray in winter."

"So it's Memphis, still."

"Yeah, Ma. Songs are like books, that way. They keep playing and keep you listening. There's always a next note, a next lick, another verse."

"I've started to read some Faulkner. He's from down that way. I guess maybe I thought he'd help me understand it all—the South, you know."

"And?"

"It's hard enough figuring out Faulkner. He writes like . . . what do they call it? Grows."

"Kudzu, Ma?"

"That's it. Kudzu. That's how Faulkner writes, but I'm making my way. It gives me a whole new shelf to read. In Faulkner's books, Memphis is a rough town, but people seem drawn to it, can't stay away. The slicks and rounders, the working women. I guess back then you could get whatever you wanted in Memphis. I guess maybe you still can." She laughs. It's good to hear her laugh.

"Well, I like your story, Ma. It's sad and uplifting all at once. A reader is a good, noble thing to be. It's sure a safer thing to be. Out here, it gets, I don't know, dicey. Complicated. Out here, the

world is a lot like Faulkner's Memphis. As for getting what you
want here, I guess it's one of those deals where you've got to be
careful about what you want."

I think she's about to ask what I want, what I've got. I think
she's about to ask if I've seen him, found him.

But she says, "We all do what we're driven to do, I've come
to realize. We're all made a certain way, Luther. There's only so
much fighting you can do against it. I was a reader and so I read.
It just so happens I could do that sitting in a chair, my legs tucked
under, that book in my hand. I'm not a reader because it's something you can do in the cold comfort of an alley. I'm a reader because of the books. If I'd needed to cross plains and swim oceans
and climb mountains to get those books, son, I'd have done it."

"So you're saying . . ."

"You're a musician and doing what musicians do. They can't
sit too long. They have to go out and scour the land for those
songs. They have to seek inspiration and a crowd to hear them.
They have to drink from life. That's not even a metaphor—that's
the big thing I've come to realize. Sometimes, it means getting
sloppy drunk from life. I know that. I suppose I always must have
known it. If being a musician just meant sitting in a chair strumming those strings for only your ears to hear, I could just look
across the kitchen and tell you this. Your grandma Sara was too
strong a woman, too stubborn of one, to accept that one little
truth. But if she hadn't been, she never would've married him. I
don't suppose, anyway. And your daddy wouldn't have been born
and I wouldn't have married him and we wouldn't have made
you. Maybe we were only meant to make you, Luther. We did a
fine, cracking job at that. You're a good man. You fight the worst
parts of that nature of yours. You think about things, wrestle with
them. You want to be a good man, a better man. Couple, three

generations down the line, a Gaunt man may be fit for proper marrying." She laughs. There's sweetness and comfort in it, hope for generations to come.

"Well, Ma."

"Yeah, Luther. Well."

"Did you mean to say, back there somewhere, that you've forgiven Daddy? I mean, that you would forgive him?"

"Well, that sure puts that theory of mine to the test, now, doesn't it, son?"

"That it does, Ma. That it does."

4

I catch a city bus going downtown. My finances are dwindling, and anyway, Memphis is not a good town for cabs. I could drive the muddy-brown Merc, but it still seems to have been misplaced.

The bus bounds down Union Avenue, passes Sun Records, looking like it did in '53 when the likes of Malcolm Gaunt and Elvis Presley poked their noses in the front door. It's a little store-front operation with an orange-red neon *S-U-N* over the door and some tourists out front posing for pictures. One steps back into the street, camera pressed to his right eye, and just about gets more than clipped by the big city bus. The driver smartly swerves as I watch out the window, thinking, *What if that tourist had bought it right then?* Sun Records as the last earthly thing that tourist saw, just before he went flat as a record. Well, I could think of a couple, three worse ways to go.

The bus goes west on Union, the city skyline rising to meet it. It's not so big, as city skylines go. *About knee-high to Delia,* I think. I don't know why I still think of her, but I do.

Downtown now, passing The Peabody hotel, the horse-drawn carriages there. The bus lurches to a stop at the corner of Union and Front. I get out.

The studio is on old Cotton Row, in a two-story stone building painted pale green. You wouldn't know there's a studio inside but for the sign that says, *Memphishine Records.*

"Hey, Luther."

"Hey, Daddy."

"This is Pete, the record mogul hereabouts."

Pete is a small, bespectacled man with a clutter of brown curly hair. He's wearing a white T-shirt with a pale green old-man sweater the color of his building. He looks at his watch and says, "Well, for a few minutes yet."

Pete gives me a tour of the studio. It's outfitted with vintage equipment from the fifties and sixties. Pete says he had to rummage the country to find it, and England, too. He's immensely proud of the place. When he says, "And England, too," it's like he swam over there and back. But I like him. He's a small, bespectacled misfit who gives himself to the songs. His best idea for having a bunch of old Memphis money at his disposal is to stuff it through the hole of an old 45 rpm record. One of Pete's knobby knees is poking through a hole in his khaki pants, as if looking to see if the coast is clear, as if his legs are about to run out of those old khaki pants and away from this little man, to see the light of day beyond the black groove of some dusty record. Pete wears old, white high-top sneakers, frayed and unlaced. He walks with a slight stoop, though he's not yet hit thirty, I bet.

I run my hand over an old microphone, thick and gray like a vault with the very soul of man inside. "Damn, Pete, this place is fine."

"But quiet," my daddy, John Gaunt, says from across the room. "What say we play?"

We sit in straight-back wooden chairs. Mine's a bit loose in the joints and I like that; it has some give, some sway. I hitch up a black electric guitar, a Gibson, and think about what my daddy said: "Every generation discovers electricity for itself." My daddy's gone electric, too; his is gold-flecked and sleek.

We hardly know each other, but there's a common language. We run through a slew of Carl Perkins songs, play Furry Lewis's old blues about those barefoot Memphis women. We play Hank's "I'm a Long Gone Daddy" as a garage rocker, a real stomper.

My daddy starts up something I don't recognize, a thumping set of chords, a steady beat that slows enough for me to hop aboard. I take up my daddy's thumping beat and nod for him to take the lead, so he does, big notes that bend and snap. It's like I'm driving a car hard and steady over smooth road and my daddy's hanging out the window, cracking whips and shooting fireworks. It's like life is some bank job we've just pulled and we haven't been caught. Not yet, anyway.

Now the road goes rough on us, throwing gravel and curves in our path. We tear down it with a righteous fury, a fool's joy, and bulletproof souls. We're riding out the song and it takes me back, to the car drifting off the shoulder where that shoulder shrugged indifference, to Buck behind the wheel but sleeping, the car taking the band for a ride.

The song bounces into the ditch and bounds out, becoming in that instant the most primitive of rocket ships. I have a brief sensation of being airborne in night sky. But gravity snatches us back and the ground punishes us for leaving. My daddy plays one wicked note that lights the room, then leaves it darker than before, and I bring the song into the station.

There's a silence in the room the floor can't support, the walls can't contain.

The next morning, he's gone. Not down to the studio—gone. "The son of a . . ."
I see the note under his coffee cup:

Dear Luther,

Well, hell, son. I guess you figured your ol' daddy'd be gone before long. Maybe those old songs we played spooked me or something. Or maybe it was that new one, the one we made up there on the spot. Yeah, I think it was that new thing. Some words came to me after. Maybe they're lyrics for the thing, I don't know. But it's a fine song as it is. Sometimes words fail and other times they just keep to themselves. I don't guess "Green Onions" needed any help, huh? I don't know what we call our song. I guess we both have our own ideas about that. But it's a fine song, no matter what you call it. I like it. The tape was rolling and Pete said he'd get you a copy. I got a copy, too. I'm going to listen to it, on my way to where I'm going.

North, you know. I figure I'll go back and try to see if maybe she'll see me. She'll refuse, probably. I hope she does. She should. Hell, my own clothes denounce me, some days. But I'm going there and I'm staying there and maybe over time—time is all I've got to my name—she'll agree to sit with me for coffee. We'll have a little moment. Maybe, over more time, we can stretch little moments like they're notes of music and we'll have us a song. We never had a song, your mother and I. You'd think being married to a musician, she'd've gotten a song if she didn't get one other thing. Surely, I'd be good for that. But the songs were all mine. I hoarded them. I stuffed them in my pockets and lined my shoes with them. They were mine—goddamn it, I made them—and I gave them away only to perfect strangers.

I was wrong. About everything, I mean. But I can't swear that I wouldn't've done it the same way all over again. How else is a musician supposed to live? The songs are out there and you have to go and get them. The songs don't walk up your walk and knock on the door. The songs don't say, "I'm here to see Mr. John." I don't know. Maybe there is another way. God's good grace to you in finding it, Luther, my son. God's grace to you. And if not God's grace, then whatever brand of grace you're drinking.

Love,

John Gaunt,
Son of Malcolm, father of Luther, husband of Molly

There's a P.S. My daddy, John Gaunt, says I'm welcome to live in the house. He says it's paid through the next month. He says Pete would love for me to hang out in the studio, for as long as it stays open. He says I could work at that like a sort of job. He says I'm good, a true talent, just maybe the best Gaunt yet. He says he's proud of his boy.

I pour a cup of coffee. I take it and my daddy's note out on the porch. It's a cold day of early winter and it looks like snow. That's what people say when the sky looks like that. It almost never does snow, though. It's like people just saying the words chases the snow away. Spooks it, seems like.

5

I set out walking. I try to find the muddy-brown Merc. I try to remember all the places I've been, retrace my stumbles. I take a city bus downtown, stop by to see Pete, but he's out front of his building, sitting on the stoop with his key in his hand, dangling from a chain.

"Hey, Pete."

"Luther."

"Your daddy shut you down?"

"Yeah, it's like that. He said he had to close the studio to make room for . . ." Pete sighs.

"For what, Pete?"

"For nothing. That's what he said. He said nothing would be a hell of a lot less of a financial drain than the noise I was up to. He called it noise."

There's a cardboard box beside him and he nudges it for-

ward. "This is for you, Luther," he says. "It's the stuff you and your
daddy cut and it's some stuff your daddy recorded before you
found him, or he found you, or however that happened. There's
also what money that I owed your daddy. He left before I could
give it to him."

"He's a long gone daddy to the end."

"Yeah, he is that. Good man, you think?"

"I don't know, Pete. But better than before, I guess."

"That's something."

"So what'll you do?"

Pete shrugs. He reaches out a hand so I can help him up.
"Go back to being rich and privileged and harmless, I reckon," he
says. "You?"

"I think I'm going to slowly ease myself into a new way of living, whatever that means," I say. "That, and try to find my damn
car."

I spend a week riding city buses, looking for the muddy-
brown Merc. One day, I end up back at my old haunt, Two Steps
From The Blues. I walk in and order a beer, served by a stocky,
middle-aged man with a southerly lean.

I play the jukebox, some piano blues by Memphis Slim.

Midway through the second one, I say, "There used to be a
woman who worked here. Her name was—"

"Ida," he says. "Still is."

"Still—"

"Still her name."

"Oh."

Memphis Slim is singing about his beer-drinking woman,
how she drank up all his pay, but I'm not convinced he wouldn't do
it all over again, if she'd give him one slim chance. Get yourself a

beer-drinking woman, boys, and be true to her. Keep her in beer
and love, play her the sad piano blues. Write songs for her.

"But anyway, she ain't here, anymore. She ain't in Memphis.
She took a—"

"She took a train?" I don't know why I'd think a girl so dismis-
sive of the sad past would blow out of Memphis on a train.

"Why, hell no, son. She took a *notion*. A damn fool notion,
you ask me. What it was, she decided to move to Atlanta, and
that's all well and good, but when she gets there she plans to
open, of all the damn fool things . . ."

He's washing a beer glass. He holds it to the light, sees a hair-
line crack, drops it in a plastic garbage can, says, "Damn."

"Of all the damn fool things, what?"

"A juke joint, of all things."

"A juke joint?"

"Yeah, you know. A blues bar, like this. 'Cept maybe with customers. Patrons. Young dudes and their beer-drinking women,
hot-shit band over yonder corner." He smiles, then the smile falls
away. "Seems working in this damn place got her hooked on the
blues. Or some damn thing did it. Seems to me that what she
woulda taken from working in this damn place is that opening a
juke joint is a damn fine way to lose what little money you got.
But you can't tell that girl a damn thing. Says she's gonna call her
place *Memphis*."

He's washing another glass. He's looking up at me. "Why the
hell you grinning, white boy?"

I string days into weeks, weeks into months. I ease myself
into a new way of living. It involves a lot of sitting and reflecting
about nothing. I take a job tending bar in a little club in Mid-
town. I hear some good music that way. Some great locals, con-

trary sorts who follow no commercial muse. A few national acts play the place, too.

There's a singer-songwriter from over Nashville way. We get to talking after his afternoon soundcheck. I pour him a beer, tell him I like his stuff. I tell him if the world was right and proper he wouldn't be playing a small club like this.

The singer says, "Well, I reckon if the world ever gets itself right and proper it'll sure know where to find me."

Then he says, "You play, barkeep?"

I say I used to, and the singer says, "No such thing as used to. You're just between songs, I bet. I mean, you pour a nice drink and all, but . . ."

"Yeah, well," I say.

And so that's how I start to play again.

There's a guitar in the back room of the club. I play late at night, after everybody clears out and the floor's been swept. I play in the early afternoon, before the night's performer comes by for soundcheck.

One night, the opening act calls in lost down somewhere in Mississippi. The owner looks at me and says, "Well?"

6

I stand on the little stage, my back to what passes for a crowd, tuning the guitar. I can see outside the picture window to the street beyond, a smattering of traffic.

I take a deep breath, sucking in dank air and cigarette fumes and the stench of a thousand last nights. I close my eyes for one slow blink, summoning in that moment my nerve and God's good grace and whatever scrap of something the fates might toss the way of the latest of the guitar-slinging Gaunts. I turn to the crowd, one foot already beating a stomp upon that little stage. I feel my hands, as if on their own, banging a fine, wild mess upon that guitar. I hear myself singing, loud enough to be heard over all that stomping and banging, loud enough to be heard six feet deep and way the hell up in the gray, besmoked North, loud like I mean it, because I do, the one about the long gone daddy.

Encore

A year later, and Delia's record is a smash. She's cold-cocked most everything else on the radio. It's number two on the charts and number one had best abdicate, if I know Delia. It's just starting to cross over from country to pop and world domination is starting to look like a distinct possibility. Delia's said to be spying other planets for conquest.

I heard she's got her own billboard in Nashville, standing hands on hips with her long legs spread way the hell up above the intersection where that main drag splits into two streets, Broadway and West End. Accidents have tripled, drivers crashing into each other, running up on sidewalks where pedestrians stand and stare. Struck dogs lie flattened like throw rugs. Delia's dressed in boots and frills and lace and she's showing a little leg. She's showing a lot of leg. It's quite a leg.

Billboard Delia's forty feet tall, a guy in a New York City bar tells me.

"Oh, actual size," I say.

The guy says, "My name's Jimmy Lee," like we've never met.

I play along; don't begrudge folks their distinctions, is how I feel about all that. Jimmy Lee's face is thinner, and pale; he looks like a rock star whose lost weekend got crossways with a month of Sundays. We shake hands. Jimmy Lee says he's a musician, says he heard me playing solo outside a café on a pawnshop acoustic.

"Sounded good," Jimmy Lee says. "But you know . . ."

"I think I do." I smile. "But why don't you tell me, just on the off chance I don't."

"You want to make noise enough for two people, what you need's another person."

"What do you have in mind? A duo?"

"No, hell. Full band," Jimmy Lee says. "I know a drummer. Doesn't say much, but keeps the beat. Name's Buck. We go way back—just met him last night in a bar. He saved my neck and this pretty face. Not this bar, but another one. Lots of bars in this town."

I say there's a lot of everything in New York. We finish our beers and head off to see a man about keeping the beat.

It's nineteen blocks to the apartment and starting to snow, but we don't mind the walk. We're drunk and running on fresh hope. A cab passes, spraying slush, but we dance out of the way. Jimmy Lee does. I fling myself to safety. I watch the flakes fall, fat asterisks disappearing onto the white sidewalk—meaning what? Whatever we decide, is what. The sidewalk is a perfect white, a blank slate. *Have at it, boy*, it seems to say. I see a song in the flakes. I see a ditty or an epic, one. Or not. The sky's a connect-the-dots puzzle, and me puzzled, happily so.

"It's been a long time. Too long," he says. "Been ages."

I don't ask what happened between Jimmy Lee and Delia. Hitching a ride with a trucker across the South, bound for the North, I heard a country-station DJ refer to Jimmy Lee in passing as Delia's ex-boyfriend and cowriter of her smash hit, "I Don't Melt." The DJ said Delia herself wrote most of the lyrics. Well. I kind of like them, no matter who wrote them.

"You think much of that song?" the trucker asked.

"Hardly ever," I said.

"Huh?" The trucker shrugged and then smiled. "Well, I like it just fine."

He said he'd like to visit Nashville sometime, he'd always loved the music. All he'd done before was drive through, plowing on with his precious cargo. He said, "You're a musician, you must know the place."

I shrugged, said, "Nah, not really." All I know about Nashville, I could have said but didn't, is that the second *l* is silent. I smile at that. The bitterness isn't in me anymore. It's left and gone, an amicable parting.

"You should go there sometime," I told the trucker.

"Take my little lady," he said. "Or somebody's." He slapped his knee.

We drove through the night, me drinking and the trucker speeding and both of us just laughing for no good goddamn reason at all. We heard Delia's song seven times between midnight and dawn.

"Yep, I like it just fine," the trucker said again. The song, he meant. Delia's song.

I was drifting a little at the time, thinking about the line of Gaunt men, thinking about my daddy trying to salvage something like love with my ma, and my daddy's daddy, who may have found something like love, or anyway the hook of his next song, with that woman he knew as Eula. I was thinking of Frankie Walls's trigger finger, of Ida Queen's long, black braids of hair and bitter wisdom and newfound love for the blues. I was thinking of the smashed bits and splinters of the old Cassandra guitar. I was thinking of how I seemed to have survived the South—or anyway had survived to have the hell beaten out of me again. I smiled at the sight of the North, gray and besmoked as ever. And I thought of the old muddy-brown Merc, wherever it was.

"A looker, I hear," the trucker said, trying to bring me back. "The girl singer."

"I mean to tell you," I said, and we laughed some more.

I tell Jimmy Lee my trucker story.

He shakes his head. "We didn't break up," he says as we pause while another cab bounds by. "I was demoted, more like. One day, I was just the guitar player in her band. Nothing was said, exactly. I handled it, you know, like a man. I went on a nuclear drunk, walked naked and nude down Music Row, tossed a neon-blue bowling ball clear through the picture window of Ernest Tubb's record store. Then I got down, begged and pleaded. I prayed. I called, sent her flowers. Then—and you might have read about this in the papers—I faked my death in her guitar-shaped pool."

"So Delia got her goddamn guitar-shaped pool," I say.

"Yeah, but she won't go near it now," Jimmy Lee says. "Not since she looked out her bedroom window and saw her guitar player in it, floating face down."

I don't ask Jimmy Lee how he faked his death. I don't want to spoil the notion that I might have been reunited with a ghost. I'm feeling rather like one myself. But in a good way, like we could walk through walls. Think of the money we'd save on cover charges alone.

"Anyway," Jimmy Lee says, "I've got a pornographic amount of royalties due me, and what's mine is yours. What's mine is ours. I say we spend it like fiends."

The walk ends at the stoop of a gray, dingy converted factory. Buck throws down a key, greets us at his apartment door with icy-cold beers with which to warm our souls. He doesn't say anything, just nods at me, but he seems glad to see me again for the first time.

I nod. *Same back at you, Buck.*

"I've got this new little start to a song," I say, strumming slowly, quietly. "It's a long story without a proper name. Goes a little something like this . . ."

Jimmy Lee falls in and takes the lead, finds a rhythm I could never conceive—a funereal jaunt, if that's possible, and I see that it is. Anything's possible when you're in a rock 'n' roll band and the night's young and the beer's cold and the world's unaware. We're as old as the ground below the dirt; we're the earth's crust and the fire beneath that bakes it; we're so new we don't have a name. Maybe we do. We'll have to see. Or maybe it's just one more thing we misplaced out on the road.

Buck falls in now, long, slow brush strokes filling in the gaps. I sing,

> *This is the story*
> *of the power chord*
> *and the glory*

It's a song about the life. It's a song about the songs. It's a little number about living to fuck up another day.

We play it until dawn and then sit on the frames of open windows, watch the snow fall. It's knee-deep and still coming. We let the ill wind wash over our sweating bodies. We tug off our shirts like it's a contest—first to double pneumonia wins. A pint bottle of Southern whiskey is passed around. Buck smacks his lips and grins. That's a soliloquy, by Buck's standards. I smile and Jimmy Lee says, "Damn, but that was good."

He's talking about the song. The whiskey goes without saying.

"But I don't think the radio'll play it," I say. "It's just not smooth, in that radio way."

Jimmy Lee takes his turn at the bottle. He rolls those eyes. "Hell with the radio," he says, but he walks over and turns it on.

It's a boom box sitting atop a piano I've been trying to play. We come in on the chorus of the song. Delia's song. But before you can say "I Don't Melt," Jimmy Lee's spinning the dial: static, the weatherman saying snow, more snow, and then the song again. And again, once more, and again. The song's everywhere. It's inescapable. So we bow to fate. We take what fate serves us and wash it down with good Southern whiskey. We listen to the words and the smooth, honeyed voice that sings them.

The song ends, then silence. It's Buck who realizes it first. Buck knows silence better than anyone; Buck picks through silence like silence is the wreckage of something once whole and golden. Jimmy Lee's about to turn off the radio, but Buck's look stops him.

The DJ comes on and says a private jet crashed in an open field somewhere in Arkansas. He says it was dark, there was ice, contact was lost. He says Delia had just played a show and there was another show to play. He says the local authorities believe—

Jimmy Lee turns off the radio and we just sit for the longest time saying nothing. We pass that bottle some more, drink, drain it. And so now we start to play. It's all we know. It's what we do. It's how we find out how we feel.

We fall into a slow one by Patsy, then another. We fire up

the Hank canon. We play the Memphis blues as New York City punk, New York City punk as Arkansas open-field country. We buy some hymns a drink.

Now the sound of Jimmy Lee's guitar, a squall that comes from the riven blue heart of ache. He gives off sparks and want and tears by the torrent. He's a foot off the ground and flying. Buck takes sticks to his silence, gives his drums a wild thumping.

I cradle the mike and think of Delia, my sweet, evil Delia. I sing a song that's stripped now of all that Nashville sheen and polish and left, like Delia's private jet, a mighty wreck as big as myth:

> *Singing, "I don't ache for your touch*
> *I just don't care that much*
> *I don't quake*
> *I don't quiver*
> *I don't swoon*
> *I don't melt*
> *when you walk in the room"*

You can hear us out on the big-city street and you can hear us clear across the country in that Arkansas open field. You can hear us deep down south of rapture, where the bad among us go. And you can hear us way the hell up in heaven, where even the high and mighty come when they're called.